AN AMISH COUNTRY TREASURE 3

RUTH PRICE

Copyright © 2015 Ruth Price

All rights reserved.

ISBN: **1522713999**
ISBN-13: **978-1522713999**

TABLE OF CONTENTS

ACKNOWLEDGMENTS	I
CHAPTER ONE	1
CHAPTER TWO	9
CHAPTER THREE	15
CHAPTER FOUR	21
CHAPTER FIVE	29
CHAPTER SIX	41
CHAPTER SEVEN	47
CHAPTER EIGHT	55
CHAPTER NINE	63
CHAPTER TEN	71
CHAPTER ELEVEN	79
CHAPTER TWELVE	87
CHAPTER THIRTEEN	93
CHAPTER FOURTEEN	101

CHAPTER FIFTEEN	109
CHAPTER SIXTEEN	115
CHAPTER SEVENTEEN	123
CHAPTER EIGHTEEN	131
CHAPTER NINETEEN	139
CHAPTER TWENTY	145
CHAPTER TWENTY-ONE	153
CHAPTER TWENTY-TWO	163
CHAPTER TWENTY-THREE	171
CHAPTER TWENTY-FOUR	181
CHAPTER TWENTY-FIVE	189
AN AMISH COUNTRY TREASURE 4	197
ABOUT THE AUTHOR	205

ACKNOWLEDGMENTS

All Praise first to the Almighty God who has given me this wonderful opportunity to share my words and stories with the world. Next, I have to thank my family, especially my husband Harold who supports me even when I am being extremely crabby. Further, I have to thank my wonderful friends and associates with Global Grafx Press who support me in every way as a writer. Lastly, I wouldn't be able to do any of this without you, my readers. I hold you in my heart and prayers and hope that you enjoy my books.

All the best and Blessings,

Ruth.

CHAPTER ONE

"But *Daed*!"

Jemima King's lovely green eyes pled with her father's implacable blue ones, but when it came to a battle of wills, it was no contest. The head of the house sputtered an incredulous *whoof*, as if he couldn't believe what he'd just heard, and Jemima quickly lowered her eyes in defeat.

But Jemima's mother dimpled, and reached out to caress her oldest daughter's cheek. "Your father said *no,* and *no* it is," she told Jemima. "But it was very sweet of you to offer. It shows that your *heart* is in the right place." Rachel met her husband's gaze, and a look of approval passed between them.

Then Jacob raised his table napkin and wiped his mouth – a signal that the discussion was over.

"Well, *that's* that! Are we ready to go?" He trained his bright eyes on Jemima's face.

She looked up at him pleadingly and made one last try. "But *Daed*! It doesn't make sense for me to give that much money to the *Yoders'*, and none to my *own* –"

Her father's answer was to slap his hands on his knees, stand up suddenly, and announce to the room at large: "Well, I'm going now! Everyone who wants to come with me had better shake a leg."

He made good on his threat immediately; he strode across the living room, opened the front door, and walked out.

Jemima's mother turned to her with a smile. "He's *proud* of you," she said softly and put her coffee cup to her lips. "And so am I."

Jemima met her eyes unhappily. "I may not be all that good. I want to give the money away, at least partly so I can see Mark and Samuel and Joseph again! All of them told me that they couldn't court with me anymore. Or at least, not while I'm so rich." She sighed, and kicked one of the table legs with a small foot.

Her mother reached for her hand. "Well, after today, everything will be back to normal," she reassured her. "When you give the money to the community fund, all of this will be behind you, and your – your *admirers* will be back over here every day, giving your father headaches."

Her mother laughed, and Jemima finally broke down and joined in. It was such a wonderful thought that she couldn't help dwelling on it – the prospect of getting this Englisch *letter business* over for good.

And getting her young men back!

She took one last sip of coffee and patted her lips with a napkin. "I guess I need to go," she sighed. "The sooner I begin, the sooner it'll be *done!*"

Jemima followed her father across the living room, and out the front door. She paused on the porch steps, and breathed in the cool morning air, and let her eyes wander over the vista.

It was overcast: low, heavy clouds scudded over the green fields and veiled the hills. The mild breeze was fragrant of rain. It was pleasantly cool, a reminder that fall wasn't far away.

But another, less pleasant sight met Jemima's eyes too: one that she hadn't expected. Instead of her father waiting patiently for her in the buggy, he was standing beside Rufus, hands on hips. He was staring at a line of cars, parked by the side of the road, about 300 yards away.

Roughly a stone's throw away.

The strangers were smart to keep their distance, Jemima thought grimly. While the trespassers had never respected her family's privacy, they'd quickly learned to respect the fact that her father was a good shot with a rock.

Jemima pinched her lips into a straight line. She could tell at once that the people in the cars were reporters. They were standing beside their opened doors, resting their cameras on the car roofs. No doubt those cameras had long-range lenses – they were probably being photographed at that very moment!

Jemima looked up at her father. She could tell that he was wrestling with the same question that was troubling her: should they cancel the trip or go to the bishop's house anyway, and arrive surrounded by a gaggle of photo-snapping reporters?

Disappointment welled up in Jemima's throat and stuck there, like a big, hard lump that would not be swallowed. She'd looked forward to this day, she had prayed for it, and now that it was here –

For the thousandth time, she wished that she had never met Brad Williams. This was *his* fault. But he hadn't stuck around to see the misery he'd caused -- the coward!

While they were standing there, another car crested the hill, passed the reporters, and stopped just outside their driveway. A small, wizened man poked his head out of the window.

Jemima's father had built an impenetrable and multi-layered barricade of old anvils, hay bales and rocks, and the man was obliged to get out of his car: but get out he did. When he skirted the barricade, Jacob strode down to meet him, calling:

"This is private property. You're trespassing -- get out!"

The man came ahead, and fixed his eyes on Jemima. He called out to her: "Are you Jemima King?"

Jemima stared at him in wonder. He was a shriveled stick of a man, with a pinched, mean face: but he had courage, she had to give him that. Anyone else would be running away by now because her father had quickened his pace and was rolling up his sleeves. But she nodded slightly.

The man pulled a sheaf of rolled-up papers out of his jacket, lobbed them at her, and turned to flee. He was surprisingly nimble, but he was obliged to dash to the hay bales – and to jump over them – to avoid being caught by her angry father.

The man landed on his feet and turned at the door of his car. "Jemima King, you've been served!" Then he tried to get back into his car, but the reporters had been watching, and some of them were nimble, too. They mobbed him before he was able to get in.

Jemima was able to hear just enough to be sure that they got the whole story out of him before he slammed the car door and sped away.

Jacob stayed at the barricade and scowled at the reporters who were brave enough to linger.

"Mr. King, is your daughter being sued?"

"Who's suing Jemima, Mr. King?"

"What's she being sued for?"

Jemima was amused to see that when her mighty father made as if to climb over the barricade, even the boldest of their tormentors fled back to the safety of their cars. His Amish beliefs notwithstanding, Jacob King was not a man to be tested.

When he was satisfied that he had chased the enemy from the field, Jacob climbed the hill again. As he came, he bent down and picked up the papers that the intruder had dropped on the lawn.

Then he handed them to Jemima.

She opened them reluctantly. They were written in very formal, very legal-sounding terms, but even she could see that the papers were telling her that she was being sued.

For $1.6 million dollars.

By a man named Caldwell C. Morton.

She looked up at her father. He put an arm around her shoulder, turned her, and walked back to the house.

"Come."

They walked back inside, and Jemima could tell by the way her father looked at her, that he expected her to burst into tears. A few months ago, she would have.

But not now.

She sighed and looked up at her father's face disconsolately. "I guess I'll stay at home today, Daed," she told him, and went to seek solitude.

CHAPTER TWO

Jemima retreated to her father's study and collapsed into his big red chair. She opened the sheaf of ominous-looking papers and flipped through them. Most of them might as well have been written in another language. She was able to glean that Caldwell C. Morton was suing her because he claimed that she'd promised to sell him the George Washington letter for $10 and was claiming that she had gone back on her word.

Yes, of course – he was the angry *Englischer*, who had tried to buy the letter from her that first day. If only she had *let* him!

Now, he was trying again to get the money, by accusing her of *lying*.

Jemima tossed the papers on the floor at her feet. Then she pulled her knees up under her chin and hugged them.

She stared into the empty grate, imagining a crackling fire. How good it would feel to burn the papers up -- and her troubles with them!

Jacob and Rachel followed softly, a few minutes after. Jacob pulled up a chair for Rachel, and another for himself. They sat down and sat with their daughter in supportive silence. Jacob's craggy face wore an uncharacteristic softness, and Rachel's doe eyes sparkled with sympathy.

After a long pause Rachel suggested: "We should pray, and ask God what to do."

Jemima didn't turn her head but instead shook it. "I already know what God wants me to do."

Rachel exchanged a wordless look with her husband, then replied: "What do you think God wants you to do, then?"

Jemima stared glumly into last year's ashes. "He wants me to keep the money." She turned to look into her mother's questioning eyes. "He wants me to *fight*. And that means I need to *get a lawyer*."

Rachel gasped audibly. Her expression plainly showed that this was the last answer she had expected.

"But you *can't!*"

Jemima set her small jaw and returned her mother's gaze. "Yes, I can," she countered, "and I will. I'm *not* a liar. That *Englischer* is the liar.

"And I've suffered too much for this money, to have someone steal it away, like a fox snatching a chicken!"

Rachel stared at her daughter in patent horror. "Jemima, it isn't *right* to resist! It's God's will for us to accept what comes, and *submit*." She turned to her husband for confirmation. "Not – not *go to court*!"

Jacob met his wife's gaze sympathetically, but his silence told his eldest daughter that he wasn't ready to agree with her. Jemima grasped the opportunity.

"I haven't joined the church yet. I can make my *own* decision," she insisted firmly.

Rachel stared at her as if she'd grown a second head. "What's come *over* you?" she wailed. "My beautiful, modest daughter – going to *court*, to *sue* a stranger over – over *money*!

"What will people think?" she cried. "What will your friends think? Oh, Mima, what will your young men say, when the girl they love goes out among the Englisch, *again*, and this time, to fight with them for *money*! They will wonder who she is. They will wonder if they still know her!" Rachel clamped her hand over her mouth in anguish.

At this, Jacob stirred. "Jemima is being sued, Rachel. She can't help *that*."

His wife turned to him. "She wants to get *rid* of the money, Jacob. She told me so herself! So why not just let the man *have* it since he wants it? Why go to court, in front of the Englisch, and, and all that nonsense with the reporters? Just let this man have the money, and –" she turned back to Jemima – "go back to living *your own life*!"

Her mother's gentle rebuke weakened Jemima's resolve. It was hard to be strong with those pleading eyes on her, and even harder to explain what she felt. But she met her mother's gaze.

"I'm *tired*, Mamm," she quavered. "I'm tired of being *bullied* over this money. And I won't let anyone call me a *liar*." She felt tears welling up, and blinked them away impatiently. "It's true that I don't want the money. I *never* wanted it. It's been nothing but a headache to me, from the first day I got it!"

"Then why not get *rid* of it?" her mother pleaded.

Jemima set her mouth. "I *am* getting rid of it," she replied. "But I believe it was God's will that I *get* that money, so I can *give* it to the people who need it, like the Yoders. Not this, this *Caldwell C. Morton*, whoever he is. He doesn't need the money. He's just greedy!"

"You don't know that," her mother objected. "God allowed this thing to happen. We should accept it."

Jemima shook her head. "But he's *suing* me. I have to go to court, and at least explain that I've given half the money away, and that part is *gone*. I gave some to the Yoders, and some to the Millers, and some to the Beilers, and a little to Grandma Sarah Fisher. And they spent it up."

Jacob looked at Rachel, and his silence was an unspoken comment. His wife shook her head and cried: "It's no use to look at me that way, Jacob King! You're not the *only* one who tries to uphold *standards in this house*!"

Then she turned to her daughter, and her usually tranquil face was wrung with anguish. "And you, Jemima – you should pray, pray *hard,* before you decide to do this thing. You'll drive away the boys who love you, *and* your friends, *and* displease God, if you turn to *fighting* and *warring.* That's the Englisch way! I can see now what this money has done to you – my poor girl!"

Then she lifted her apron to cover her face, and fled upstairs, weeping. Jacob gave Jemima a long, but sympathetic look before leaving the room to follow her.

Jemima sighed and fell into a depressed silence. But to her surprise, Deborah had been listening from the doorway. She walked out into the study, munching an apple. She looked at Jemima steadily.

"Don't let it faze you," she said. "It's your money. I say, *fight* the sucker."

Then she drifted off again, leaving Jemima to stare after her.

CHAPTER THREE

A faint tapping disturbed Jemima's dream. She turned her head on the pillow, murmuring, but she couldn't recapture it. The dream slid away from her, and slowly formed again.

Only this time, it became the darkness of her bedroom.

Moonlight slanted in through the window. There was no sound except for the faint echo of her father's thunderous snoring, from far down the hall. Jemima turned, sighing, and settled into her pillow again.

But the tapping came again. This time, sharp and loud, like something hitting her window.

She opened her eyes. It *was* something hitting her window.

Her heart began beating oddly. *Someone was outside on the lawn.* Was it a reporter, or, some crazy stranger, or even –

She frowned and set her mouth, and threw the covers back. She put two bare feet on the bare floor, threw a knitted shawl around her shoulders, and went to the window.

The moonlight flooded the lawn below with light. A man was standing below her window, looking up.

It – it looked like *Joseph Beiler*!

For an instant, astonishment wiped every other thought out of Jemima's mind. Joseph Beiler, on her lawn at midnight? He was the shyest boy she had ever known. Something was surely wrong! The sudden fear that something terrible had happened, urged her to dress quickly, and go down to meet him.

When she opened the screen door and stepped out onto the porch, he was standing at the corner of the house, waiting for her. She moved quickly down the porch steps, and across the lawn to meet him.

She searched his face anxiously. "Why, Joseph, what's wrong?" she whispered. "Why are you here? Has something *bad* happened?"

To her amazement, his answer was to grab her by the shoulders, crush her to his chest, and give her the third-wildest kiss of her young life. Her eyebrows shot up, but after the shock wore off, she didn't make a serious effort to get out of his arms. To her amazement, it seemed that Joseph wasn't *nearly* as shy as he seemed. He was actually an *excellent* kisser -- when he applied himself.

When he released her, she paused to catch her breath, and looked up at him. "Why, *Joseph*! I'm surprised at you!"

He seemed to take her breathless comment as a rebuke. He hung his handsome head, and said, softly: "I'm sorry, Jemima. I know what I said. But I couldn't stay away. I had to see you!"

Jemima smoothed her hair, and tried not to smile. "I understand, Joseph."

He took her hand warmly. "I *knew* you'd forgive me." The thought seemed to overwhelm her gentle suitor. He looked down at the ground.

"I shouldn't have come. I still stand by what I said before."

"Oh, I know, Joseph – and I *understand*. I mean to give away the money, and I understand that we can't see each other until it's gone. But it may be a while, Joseph. Something else has happened, and there may be a – a delay."

He looked down into her face. "What delay?"

She nodded unhappily. "A man came by the house and gave me papers. He said that I'm being sued for all the money by a strange Englischer. The Englischer says that I promised to sell him the letter, and lied!"

Joseph said nothing, but seemed shaken by a burst of anger. He pulled her close in a protective embrace, and pressed his cheek tight against hers. He rumbled angrily: "*Er ist verrückt!*" and for an instant, the deep bass note almost reminded Jemima of her father.

"Now I have to go to court and tell them that I don't have all the money anymore," Jemima whispered. "I've given almost half of it away already."

Joseph pressed her close. "My beautiful *maus*, don't be afraid. I'm here for you, don't let it make you afraid." Joseph kissed her brow, and tightened his hold around her.

Jemima allowed herself to be comforted. Joseph was tall and muscular and sweet and strong. He had silky brown hair and beautiful brown eyes, like a deer. His skin was tan and his teeth were white. And after all she'd been through in the last few days, Joseph's arms were a very welcome haven.

Jemima snuggled into them, thinking that Joseph really was, overall, the best-looking of all her suitors, and certainly the most sensitive. And after that astounding kiss, he had *a third* thing in his favor.

Now if he would only confess that he *loved her,* and give up writing poetry, she could see herself...

"I'll stand by you, Mima, no matter what you decide to

do," he told her suddenly. "Even if you go to court!"

Jemima looked up at him, startled out of her thoughts. "*Really,* Joseph?"

He nodded. "Yes, Mima," he said simply, and closed his eyes in a determined frown. "It isn't fair that you should suffer any more than you *have*."

Jemima looked up at him hopefully. Maybe *now* Joseph was going to do more than kiss her. Maybe he was going to tell her that he *loved* her. Maybe he was even going to *make himself vulnerable.*

"I'll go to the courthouse with you, if you like," he told her, opening his eyes again. "I'll help you find a lawyer, if you want one."

Jemima stared at him in the darkness, crestfallen. She had hoped that Joseph, of all people, would say *something* at least about love. Why did men always refuse to share what they felt?

She shook her head and tried to bring her mind back to what he was saying.

"That's wonderful of you, Joseph," she replied, "but my father will help me -- I think."

Joseph looked down at her. "Then promise you'll tell me as soon as the way is clear," he whispered. "Every day apart from you feels like a lifetime!"

Jemima's hope revived. "Oh, Joseph, that's so *sw*..."

But he turned and kissed her again so delightfully that Jemima quite lost her train of thought. In fact, she lost even the desire that Joseph would share his heart, just so long as he didn't *stop*.

Eventually Joseph pulled back from her, and cupped her face in his big hands. "I'll go with you to the courthouse, Mima," he smiled. "I'll be there for my *maus*, to lend her strength.

"And then, when all this nightmare is over -- we can get *married*!"

CHAPTER FOUR

Jemima was silent at the breakfast table the next morning. So was her mother, who showed distressing signs of having spent the night in tears; and also her father, whose sagging shoulders suggested that he had also been up late, trying to console her.

They ate in heavy silence, except for Deborah, who filled the void by complaining about the lack of discipline at school. Deborah said that she'd been the target of hateful boys who had suggested that she needed "a broom and a black hat."

"I don't know what they're *talking* about," she exclaimed, extending her hands. "*No one* is more patient than I am!"

This startled Jemima out of her depression, and she lifted her eyes in wonder to her sister's face. It seemed to irritate Deborah even further.

"What are *you* staring at, fright wig? And stop chewing your nails – you look like a four-year-old!"

It was a measure of their parent's preoccupation, that no one corrected Deborah for this rudeness or made the slightest mention of the woodshed: a fact that Jemima noted with some bitterness. But she had more important things to think about, than *Deborah*.

She had already decided to go find a lawyer and had planned to ask her father to drive her to town; but one look at her mother's face told Jemima that her father wouldn't be helping her *that* day.

She could drive the buggy herself, but it would be risky. The reporters could reappear at any time.

The thought occurred to her that she could ask Joseph to drive her into town, since he supported her decision: but his family's farm was clear across the valley, not close at all. And anyway, she didn't want Joseph to press her to *marry him* again. She couldn't make such a big decision when her life was upside down, and she'd told him so last night. But he hadn't paid much attention.

Maybe she could *walk* to town unnoticed, if she cut across country instead of using the road. Of course it would be a long, tiring trip, but the corn was tall in every field, and it would keep her out of sight, most of the way.

Yes, *that* was the best.

Jemima rose from the table, picked up a basket, and went outside to *pretend* that she meant to do her daily chores: gathering eggs, and vegetables, and working in the garden. But when she saw that no one was watching, she turned and walked out into the garden. She kept walking into the bushes at the edge of the garden, and through the woods beyond, all the way to the fence at the edge of their property.

Jemima looked this way and that, hiked up her skirt, and climbed over the rail fence. That put her into their neighbors' corn field, the first of many on the way to town. Jemima walked into it and was instantly swallowed up in the green rows.

After having been in the spotlight for so many months, there was something deliciously secretive about disappearing into the fields – going where *no one* could find her. Once she was inside the cornfield, there was nothing ahead, to either side or behind, except green stalks stretching into infinity.

And it was a beautiful day for walking -- a fine, bright morning, with the high white clouds of late summer sailing over the earth. Jemima stopped now and then to shade her eyes, and look up at them through the waving green leaves. She saw and heard nothing else, except the faint call of birds, and the equally faint hum of farm equipment somewhere across the valley. Occasionally her approach startled some small animal. A rabbit that she hadn't guessed was there suddenly jumped into the air and rocketed away: and a field mouse scurried across her path and disappeared.

They were the only living things she saw for a long while.

Halfway through her route, she climbed over a pasture fence and crossed over into the Christener's fields. The land belonged to Mark's family, and Jemima played with the idea of paying a quick visit, but decided against it. Mark had made it clear that he didn't plan to see her again until she had resolved this issue.

She crossed the entire breadth of the Christner's corn field without incident, but when she stepped out of it and prepared to cross the fence to the farm next door, she was mortified to see Mark standing not ten yards away – staring.

"*Oh!*" she shrieked and climbed down from the fence.

Mark's expression was as puzzled as his voice. "*Mima?* What are you doing way out here?" He put down a pair of pliers and took off his work gloves. Jemima noticed, with deep embarrassment, that she had managed to pop out of the field at the very point at which Mark had been mending their fence.

A full-body wave of heat began to crawl up from her toes. "I—that is – I'm walking to *town*."

Mark looked at her doubtfully. "Through the *fields*?"

Jemima nodded and looked down at her feet.

There was a heavy silence. Mark finally shrugged and sat down on a tree stump. "What's wrong, Mima? You'd never go hiking across country unless something was *bad* wrong. What is it?"

Jemima bit her lip and looked at him unhappily. "I'm going to town to get a *lawyer*," she murmured.

Mark's dark eyebrows shot up. "A lawyer? *You*? Are you in some kind of trouble?"

Jemima turned pleading eyes to his face. "Yes – big trouble! An Englischer is suing me for all the money I have! A man came and gave me papers and said I had to appear in court! The Englischer claims that I promised to sell him the George Washington letter – *and that I lied*!"

Mark's brow gathered darkness. He stood up, came over, and put his arms around her. Jemima pillowed gratefully on his chest.

"Mamm is unhappy with me," she murmured. "She says I should just let him have the money, but I *can't,* because I've already given half of it away! And if I don't fight, it's like admitting that he was right and that I'm a *liar*!"

"No one who knows you could *ever* think such a thing, Mima," Mark assured her, and kissed her cheek. "And it doesn't *matter* what outsiders think."

Jemima frowned. "It matters to me!" she said and pulled out of his arms. "And I'm not going to let him just *take* this money from me when he has no right, and when God *told* me to give it to others. It isn't fair!"

Mark's eyes were dark and troubled. "I think your Mamm is right, Mima," he said slowly. "I think you should let the Englischer have the money. It would end this trouble, and everything could go back to normal again. Don't you want that?"

Jemima felt her lower lip trembling and bit it. "Oh, of *course* I do!" she cried, "but not like *this*! I won't have people saying that I *lie* when I can prove that I *didn't*. And I won't let this greedy man come and steal from me!"

Mark ran a hand through his black hair and sighed. "All right then, Mima, have it your way. But I still think you'd do better to let be.

"And you still haven't told me -- *why* are you in our cornfield?"

This time, the tears were dangerously close. "Because we can't go out of our house!" Jemima cried. "There are reporters parked on the road outside our driveway, waiting for me like *vultures*! And Daed won't drive me because Mamm is upset! I don't want to drive *alone*, and if I walk through the fields, maybe they won't see me, and I can go to town in *peace*!"

Mark gave her a look that said he saw the tears underneath, and he took her in his arms again and kissed her hair. "All right, Mima. Come inside with me, and have something to eat, and rest. Let me change out of my work clothes, and I'll drive you into town if you're determined to go."

"Yes, I *am*. Thank you, Mark," she replied doggedly, but the tears trembling just underneath her words pooled up in her eyes and formed a knot in her throat. She was grateful that Mark asked her no more questions. Grateful that he just held her until knot had loosened somewhat and she could breathe without embarrassing herself.

CHAPTER FIVE

Jemima followed Mark back to the big white farmhouse that had been built by his great-great-grandfather 100 years before. It was white, with a green roof, spotlessly clean, and, apparently, temporarily empty.

Mark's mother Elizabeth was out doing chores and was nowhere to be seen: so Mark invited Jemima to sit down at the kitchen table. He poured her a cup of coffee, served her a piece of *snitz* pie, grabbed one for himself, and then went upstairs to change.

Jemima ate the pie gratefully. It was past noon now, and the walk had made her hungry.

When Mark came back downstairs, he was holding a big bonnet. He held it out to Jemima. "This belongs to my Mamm. If you wear it, no one will be able to see your face." Then he went outside to hitch up the buggy.

A few minutes later they were riding down the driveway and out onto the road.

They sat in silence. It was a good five miles to town from the Christner's farm, and Mark, as always, preferred silence to speech. But to Jemima's relief, it was the comfortable silence of long friendship. Even though the money had put a barrier between them, the money was still the only barrier there was.

It was also apparent that the bonnet was doing its job. It was far too big for Jemima and hid her face completely if she turned away from the road. No one they passed on the road took a second look at her. If they knew Mark, they supposed her to be his mother: if they didn't know Mark, they probably thought the same. Jemima figured that since the reporters didn't know him, they'd see him as just another young Amish man. But she was careful to look away when cars passed by, and to her great gratitude, no one took any notice of them.

Mark drove her, via sleepy side streets, to the office of Barfield Hutchinson, a lawyer who was trusted and sometimes hired by Amish folk in the area. Jemima had chosen him because he was frankly the only lawyer she knew and because she had once heard her father speak of him approvingly.

When Mark stopped the buggy outside his office, he threw the reins aside, turned to her, and took her hands solemnly.

"Mima, are you *sure* about this? Maybe you should think about it some more. This is a big step."

Jemima looked into his frowning eyes. She knew he was genuinely worried for her.

"You're so sweet, Mark," she whispered, and kissed him. His lips were warm and strong and delicious on hers – they tasted of snitz pie, and *protective*. But when they parted, she looked him dead in the eye.

"I've decided. I am going in there, and I -- I am going to *hire* him. I have no *choice*."

Mark sighed, and shook his head. "You're changing, Mima," he murmured, half to himself, and Jemima shot him a frightened look. Her mother's warning came back to her with terrible force, and she was shaken by the sudden fear that she might *lose* Mark.

"You don't hate me – do you, Mark?" she whispered.

He looked shocked. "Of course not, Mima," he sputtered and leaned in to kiss her reassuringly. "Hate you! Never. It's just that – well, you never used to be this – *brave*."

Jemima digested this and decided that she would take it as a compliment. "I've *had* to be," she told him grimly, then gathered her skirts, and climbed down from the buggy.

Mark opened the door for her, and they walked into the lawyer's office. It was housed in a two-story red brick building, the kind found in any small town square -- except this one was on a tree-lined side street.

The interior was elegantly furnished in colonial antiques – a highly polished grandfather clock ticked softly in one corner, what looked like a Persian rug covered the floor, and even the lobby furniture was upholstered in leather.

Jemima looked uncertainly at Mark, and he took her elbow. They walked to the receptionist's desk.

A young, attractive Englisch woman sat there. She was well-groomed and well-dressed but didn't seem especially well-disposed toward visitors. She smiled politely – but coolly, Jemima was quick to note.

"Good afternoon. Can I help you?"

Jemima nodded. "I'd like to hire Mr. Hutchinson," she said firmly.

The woman smiled broadly, and Jemima went red to the roots of her hair.

"Do you have an *appointment*?" she asked blandly.

Jemima shook her head.

The young woman smiled again. "I'm afraid Mr. Hutchinson is busy today," she said smoothly, "but if you'd like to make an appointment, he might be able to see you---" she glanced at her desk calendar "– two weeks from Friday."

Jemima looked at Mark helplessly. His lips were pressed into a thin, straight line. He said nothing, but he took hold of the bonnet and gently lifted it from her head.

The woman looked up and froze. Her eyes widened.

"This is *Jemima King*," Mark told her.

The woman stared, and then recovered her poise. She smiled again, and this time the expression touched her eyes.

"Let me buzz Mr. Hutchinson," she said. "I'm sure he'll want to see you, Miss King." She picked up the phone and pressed a button.

"Mr. Hutchinson, there's a *Miss Jemima King* to see you." She looked up at Jemima's face. "*Yes*. All right."

She put the phone down again. "Mr. Hutchinson will be right with you."

Jemima glanced at Mark gratefully, but she had no time to do more. There was a faint bumping sound on the other side of a polished door, and it opened to admit Mr. Barfield Hutchinson. He was a tall, distinguished-looking elderly man, with a thick head of long white hair, bright blue eyes, a trim mustache, and a broad, handsome mouth.

He smiled to reveal a full set of white teeth, and gestured in welcome.

"Please come *in*," he smiled.

They walked into his spacious office, and Jemima sank into one of two seats facing an ornate antique desk. The wall behind the desk was covered in law books that looked as if they dated back a century at least.

Mr. Hutchinson sat down in his leather chair, folded his hands on top of his desk, leaned forward, and smiled at Jemima.

"Now what can I do for *you*, Miss King?"

Jemima glanced over at Mark, but if she had hoped for encouragement, she was disappointed. Mark's stoic expression told her that he still thought their visit was a mistake, and that he wished neither of them was there. She set her mouth and turned to the lawyer.

"I want to hire you," she told him. "I'm being *sued*."

"Ah." The smiled faded from Mr. Hutchinson's face, to be replaced by an expression of mild concern. "And *who* would be suing such a charming young lady?"

Jemima dug into her bag and pulled out the sheaf of legal papers. She handed them to Mr. Hutchinson. "A man named Caldwell C. Morton," she frowned.

The lawyer took the papers and scanned them. He

mumbled under his breath and flipped the pages briefly. "*Hmm*. Yes, I've heard your story, Miss King, like most everyone else in the country." He looked up at her and smiled. "Congratulations on your historic find! Do you have any proof that you purchased the letter, to establish ownership – a receipt, witnesses?"

Jemima nodded. "I bought the letter at Mr. Satterwhite's Gift Shop on the square," she told him, "and I think I still have the receipt. I'll have to look. But Mr. Satterwhite sold the clock to me, so he knows I bought it. And there was someone else, who saw me take it out of his shop, and who saw the letter fall out of it."

"Who would that be?" the lawyer asked, scribbling on a notepad.

Jemima felt herself going red. She was very conscious of Mark, sitting at her elbow. She coughed a little. "A reporter, from the *Ledger* newspaper, named Brad Williams."

The lawyer nodded. "Yes, of course. The young man who broke the story! It's been very well documented, so I don't think I need to get that part of it from you."

Jemima looked down at her hands, and could *feel* Mark scowling.

"And – forgive me, Miss King –" the lawyer was smiling again – "but just for the record, are you certain that you never signed anything to the effect that you would sell the clock or the letter to this Morton fellow? You never promised that, in any way?"

Jemima shook her head vehemently. "*No*. He asked me over and over, but I never signed anything, and I never promised him I would. He's *lying*!"

"Is there anyone who can back you up on that, in court?"

Jemima bit her lip and looked down at her hands again. "Yes," she replied unwillingly. "After I bought the clock, the Englischer came out to my house and asked to buy it. Then Brad Williams came out, too. He told me that the clock could be valuable, and *not* to sell. Then the Englischer threw money on the porch and demanded I sell the clock to him. And said I had *promised* to sell. And I told him that no, I had *not* promised to sell, only to show him the clock. And – and Brad Williams was there when I said that."

Mr. Hutchinson scribbled again. "Good."

Jemima raised fierce eyes to his face. "But I don't want you to call Brad Williams, or to talk to him at all because I don't want to see him again!"

The lawyer looked at her. "Why not, Miss King? It seems to me that he could help you a great deal."

Jemima felt suddenly flustered, and huffed, "*Because,* because he was the one who got me into this mess, and I never want to see him again!"

The lawyer looked down and scribbled again. "I respect your wishes, Miss King, but I'm bound to tell you that it will make my job harder if he doesn't appear. Assuming he was the only witness to that conversation?"

Jemima bit her lip and nodded.

Mr. Hutchinson sighed. "Well, Miss King, I'll *still* be happy to represent you. Try hard to find the receipt, and if you do, send it to me."

"There's something else," Jemima told him reluctantly. "I don't have all the money any more. I've given it away to different people. I only have half of what he's suing me for!"

The lawyer paused, pulled his glasses down his nose, and stared at Jemima over them. "You mean to say – you've *given away* half of the money?"

Jemima looked down, and nodded.

"Do you mind telling me – to *whom*?"

Jemima looked up at him uncomfortably. "Well – to the Yoders – their little boy fell down a well, and broke almost all his bones, and he was in the hospital, and they couldn't pay their bills, so I gave them $200,000. And then there was the Millers, John Miller had a heart attack in January and the family's bills were terrible, and I gave them $150,000 for that. And I gave about as much to the Beilers for their premature baby, and a little to Grandma Sarah Fisher for her last trip to the emergency room, when she had the mini-stroke and had to stay overnight."

Mr. Hutchinson frowned, and closed his eyes, and shook his head slightly. "So – you're telling me – you gave all of that money to *other people*?"

Jemima met his eyes. "Yes."

"Would they be willing to be deposed?"

Jemima shook her head, and he added: "Would they come and tell me that themselves if they knew it would help you?"

Jemima nodded. "I think so."

Mr. Hutchinson tilted his head, and added: "You've certainly been very generous, Miss King! Would you tell me, please, how much of this money you've spent on *yourself*?"

Jemima raised her eyebrows and shrugged. "Why, *nothing*. I'm healthy, and my family does well. I don't need *anything*.

"But do – do you think I'm in very much trouble?"

Mr. Hutchinson smiled again, very broadly. "Oh, my dear," he told her, "don't worry about *anything*. Just leave everything to me." He rubbed his long hands and muttered, half to himself: "Morton will probably drop the suit, because if we go to a jury trial, I'll *destroy* him."

Mr. Hutchinson looked up at Jemima and smiled again. "What I mean to say is, of course I'll do everything in my power to see that you prevail."

CHAPTER SIX

Jemima moved uncomfortably in the buggy seat as they drove back from town. It seemed to her that the *tone* of Mark's silence had changed. On the way into town, his silence had been peaceful and relaxed. After their visit to the lawyer's office, she sensed -- something *else.*

After a while she turned to Mark and asked: "*What?*"

He looked away, out over the fields. To her relief, he didn't ask what she meant.

"I hate to hear you talk about that Williams Englischer," he blurted. "I hate to think of the two of you together."

Something about the way he said it melted Jemima's heart.

Poor Mark! She reached out and grasped one of his hands.

"You don't need to worry, Mark," she told him softly. "I didn't like having to talk about Brad Williams, either -- I wish I'd never *met* him.

"If it makes you feel better -- sometimes I really think that I *hate* him!"

Mark glanced at her, with a look almost like pain. "That's what I mean, Mima," he murmured. "It *doesn't* make me feel better, because – that's *new*. I've never seen you like that before."

Jemima pulled back her hand and sighed. "That's because no one has caused me so much *harm* before!" she replied.

"So that's what it is, Mima?" he asked. "Anger? I need to know. Because every time you talk about him, you look – I don't know – *stirred up*."

"You'd be stirred up, too, if he'd done this to *you*!" Jemima answered tartly, and then almost gasped aloud -- because she sounded so much like *Deborah*. But to her relief, Mark sputtered out a reluctant laugh.

"Fair enough. I know you have good cause to be mad at him." He turned to look at her. "But I'd hate to think that he'd gotten to you somehow, Mima."

Jemima raised her eyes to his and held them. "*Why*, Mark?" she asked pointedly.

He shrugged. "I just *would*, that's all."

"*Oh*."

Jemima hoped that Mark would hear the disappointment in her voice, and understand what it meant. It was one thing to be reserved. But if you were a *lover*, sooner or later you needed to *say so*.

She toyed with the idea of just – telling him that. But instead, she lapsed into silence herself and gazed out over the cornfields as they passed.

When they reached the Christener farm, Jemima would have walked home, but Mark wanted to walk back with her. She tried to object – she felt guilty about interrupting his day – but he insisted. So she waited while he unhitched the buggy, and put the horse back in its stall, and returned to her.

They walked back the way she had come, though Mark did twitch his mouth to one side, and say that it felt strange to be in a field without a *team of horses*. Jemima laughed because it was funny, and when he held out his hand, she took it.

They walked back to her home hand in hand, as they had sometimes done when they were children, and to Jemima it felt natural and right. They said nothing because they didn't need to talk to feel comfortable, but she enjoyed his company and knew that he enjoyed hers.

That was the thing about Mark: he was so *easy* to be with. He made no demands on her, and yet he was always there, sensible, strong and reliable. He made no attempt to entertain her, but she felt no need to be entertained. They just *liked* each other and were comfortable together, and it was enough.

When they finally reached the fence that bordered her parent's farm, Mark lifted her in his arms and sat her down on the topmost rail of the fence. He held her there with his hands and looked into her questioning eyes.

"I think it was a wonderful thing you did, Mima. Giving all that money away to the Yoders, and the others. The man was right. That was very generous."

Jemima smiled, and looked down, and went pink. Mark's praise pleased her out of all proportion.

Because Mark had never been one to gush – when he praised you, he *meant* it.

"It's your rumspringa. You could've spent all that money on yourself, on a car, or a trip somewhere, or lots of pretty Englisch clothes." He raised a brown hand and brushed a tendril of hair back from her brow. "You would look so beautiful then, that *no one* could resist you."

"Oh, Mark!" she sputtered and shook her head, but he didn't back down.

"It's true, Mima. You're the most beautiful girl I've ever met. The most beautiful girl I ever expect to meet. And not just on the outside."

Jemima became very still. She raised her eyes to Mark's, searched them, hoped that he'd say the words that *should* come next.

The dappled sunlight played over his shoulders, turned his hair to black silk tinged with blue. His eyes were dark as sapphires, ringed with a smudge of black lashes. He smiled faintly and leaned in to kiss her, soft and sweet and warm.

Jemima received his kisses gratefully, savored them for the precious things they were, rolled them over her tongue like a favorite taste. But to her disappointment, Mark *still* did not use his tongue to form the words she longed to hear.

He pulled back from her at last, and kissed her again just on the edge of her mouth, and played with her ear.

"I want you to ask you something, Mima," he said quietly. "When all of this is over, and things have settled down, I'm going to come back to your house and ask you a question. I think you know what it's going to be. I want you to promise me you'll think about it, in the meantime."

Jemima felt a strange sensation: love and exasperation, simultaneously.

Exasperation won -- slightly. She spoke kindly but gave him an arch look. "How do I know what to think about, when you won't even tell me what the *question* is?"

Mark smiled but shook his head. "Don't play with me, Mima. I'm serious." He looked up into her eyes. "Promise."

Her exasperation melted. It was impossible to resist those beautiful blue eyes.

"*I promise*, Mark," she whispered.

"It wouldn't hurt, if you promised not to say *yes* to anyone else, before you talk to me," he added, only half-jokingly.

Jemima met his eyes and smiled apologetically. "There *are* other boys who are asking me -- *questions*," she confessed. "It's only fair you should know."

He twisted his mouth down. "I'd have to be pretty dumb not to guess," he told her wryly. "But I do have a chance, don't I, Mima?"

Jemima looked up at him, startled. "Of course you do – Oh, *Mark*!" She took him in her arms and hugged him. "How could you think any *different*?"

She could feel him relax. He put his arms around her and kissed her one last time.

"That's all I wanted to know, Mima," he told her. And before she could answer, he had released her and had disappeared into the rustling leaves.

CHAPTER SEVEN

When Jemima returned home, it was already late afternoon. She hurried to finish the chores she had left undone and tiptoed back into the house. To her relief, her mother was busy cooking dinner, and her father was still out in his workshop, and there was no sign of Deborah.

Her mother was standing at the kitchen sink. Jemima quietly piled the vegetables on the kitchen table, and would have crept upstairs, when her mother said, without turning:

"You went to the lawyer today, didn't you, Jemima?"

Jemima froze and hung her head. "Yes."

Rachel nodded, still without turning, and Jemima knew

without having to look that she was fighting tears.

"It's your decision. You're on your rumspringa, and you're free to choose. I just wanted to let you know that…I am *not* upset with you."

Jemima looked up at her. "You're *not*?"

Her mother took a deep breath and nodded, "Everything is all right. Go upstairs and wash up for supper. It's almost done."

Jemima batted back quick tears of her own. Hurting her gentle mother was the *last* thing she wanted to do. And it was the first time, ever in her *life*, that she had gone against her wishes.

But on the other hand, she saw no way to do differently than she *had* done so it would be dishonest to apologize. She stared at her mother's back unhappily.

"*Thank you, Mamm*," she murmured and fled upstairs.

That evening dinner was subdued, but not as uncomfortable as Jemima had feared. Her mother was as good as her word, and her father was unchanged. Jemima suspected that he agreed with her decision, deep down: but in any case, he didn't scold her, except to ask how she had gotten to town.

Jemima told him, quite truthfully, that she had walked, and

had gone across country. Her father raised his bushy red eyebrows, and told her not to go alone next time: but said no more than that -- and she was grateful.

Deborah, however, was worse than ever. She complained about the food, accused Jemima of running off to meet boys instead of going to the lawyer's, and even talked back to Rachel when she rebuked her for her rudeness.

This stirred up her father's parental wrath, and to Jemima's guilty satisfaction, he took Deborah by the back of her apron and pulled her out to the front porch. Rachel and Jemima picked at their food and pretended not to hear the sounds of repeated *thwacks*, their father's booming voice, delivering a lecture, and Deborah's howls.

Jemima cleared her throat. "Do you think it will do any good this time?" she whispered.

Her mother pinched her lips into a straight line, and shook her head. "I *hope* so." The sound of renewed howls, interspersed with curses, assaulted their ears.

She returned Jemima's glance. "*Pray* for your sister."

Jemima raised her brows and thought that she would rather pray to be delivered *from* her sister: and immediately felt guilty for the uncharitable thought.

For a few days afterward, Jemima enjoyed relative peace.

Her parents, apparently having agreed to extend the olive branch, said no more to her about the lawyer; her suitors gave her rest; and Deborah, no doubt fearing retribution, maintained a resentful and much-appreciated silence.

Then one day Samuel Kauffman came knocking at the door.

Jemima was sitting in the living room, trying to soothe her jangled nerves by working on a quilt. Her mother had suggested that it might help her to work on something that required her concentration, and so far that morning it had worked.

But then there was a soft knock on the screen door, and when she looked up and saw Samuel standing there, so tall and handsome, every other thought flew out of her head. He had taken off his hat, and his beautiful blonde hair reminded her of wheat waving in the sun.

"Can I come in, Jemima?" he asked.

She dimpled and stood up immediately, and the quilt fell forgotten to the floor. "Of course, Samuel! What a question!"

He seemed unusually subdued – he didn't even smile -- but Jemima was so glad to see him that she didn't care. She gathered up the quilt and threw it over a chair.

"Come and sit with me." She sat down on the sofa and patted it.

Samuel came and sat down immediately, and she noticed that he was holding something. It looked like a newspaper, and that was odd because most people she knew didn't read Englisch newspapers.

But he set it down on the couch and turned to her. He took her hands in his and looked at her as if someone had died.

Jemima's smile faded. "Why, Samuel, what is it? You look as if something *terrible* has happened!"

His blue eyes searched hers. "I need to ask you a question, Mima," he said gravely.

Jemima's heart jumped into her throat. She couldn't trust herself to speak, but nodded, looking up at him expectantly.

He looked down at her hands as if he was gathering his nerve, and then said: "Joseph Beiler is going around town telling everyone that the two of you are – are *engaged*. Is it true, Mima?"

Jemima felt her mouth dropping open. "*Engaged*?"

"Everyone in the valley is talking about it. But – but I had to hear it from *you*. Is it true, Mima?"

Jemima felt her face going warm. Joseph *never* listened very well. She had told him that she needed time to *think*, not that she agreed to *marry* him! Poor Joseph, he was too much of a romantic, he always let his hopes outrun…

She remembered Samuel and bit her lip. "No, Samuel, it

isn't true," she told him firmly. "It's true that Joseph asked me to marry him, and that I promised to *think* about it, but I haven't given him any answer yet."

Samuel relaxed visibly. He closed his eyes briefly and leaned back against the couch, and revived. For the first time since he walked in, he smiled – a little ruefully, but with the same charm as always.

"I should've known," he confessed, running a hand through his hair. "Joseph gets carried away. But Mima, you – you couldn't say *yes* to anyone but me – *could* you?"

He grinned again, with that boyish charm, and Mima laughed in spite of his cheeky joke. She knew him well enough to know that he *was* making a joke – Samuel never took *anything* too seriously -- even himself.

But his question sent a wave of delight coursing through her. She looked down primly. "Why, Samuel, are you asking me to marry you?" she smiled.

When she ventured to look up again, Samuel's face looked startled. He cracked a confused grin, and then broke out into infectious laughter. "Yes, I guess I *am*!" he admitted, and Jemima had to smile with him. Samuel was *so* adorable – if she married him, her life would be full of fun and laughter, because he was so full of mischief – and so *terribly* handsome.

He pressed her hands between his, and became serious

again. His bright blue eyes questioned her. "*Will* you marry me, Mima?" he asked.

Jemima looked up at him, and as soon as their eyes met, he kissed her. It wasn't the playful, exploratory kisses that he usually gave her, and that she loved. It was a sober, serious kiss, full of the love that Samuel had never been able to bring himself to *say* but had never failed to *show*.

When their lips parted, Jemima looked up at him longingly but shook her head. "I can't answer you now, Samuel," she said softly. "I need time to pray and to think. But something *bad* has happened, and I'm so caught up in it, I *can't* think. I can hardly even *pray!*"

Samuel looked crestfallen, and her heart went out to him, but she had no other answer to give.

He nodded, and then reached for their town newspaper. "The *something bad* -- does it have anything to do with *this*?" he asked.

Jemima looked down at it. To her horror, there on the front page was the blaring headline: *Local Girl Center of $1.6 Million Lawsuit*.

She clapped a hand over her mouth and felt her self-control begin to slide away. Samuel's expressive eyes radiated compassion, and he took her in his arms.

"It never *ends,* Samuel!" she told him hopelessly, and he whispered comfort as she broke down and gave full vent to her feelings.

CHAPTER EIGHT

Delores Watkins sauntered into her star reporter's office and tossed a newspaper down on his desk with a *plop*. She tilted her head, put one hand on her hip, and drawled: "Do you mind telling me why I had to see this in some *other* newspaper? I thought this was your signature story, wonder boy!"

Brad Williams had a phone to his ear, but he swiveled in his chair and picked up the paper. It was a copy of the *Lancaster Farmer's Friend*, the tiny community paper from Serenity, Pennsylvania. The headline read: *Local Girl Center of $1.6 Million Lawsuit.*

Brad frowned and spoke hurriedly into his phone. "I have

to go. I'll call you back." He pushed the mic arm up and scanned the story.

"Somebody's suing *Jemima King*?" He looked up into Delores' ironic brown eyes and snapped his fingers at her. "*I know who it is* – it's that guy who was trying to buy the letter off her! Am I right?"

"Congratulations, Sherlock," Delores replied dryly. "It's the second graf down."

"What is this – *this morning's* edition? Has anybody else seen this yet?" he asked.

"I don't know," she replied. "But I do know *this*: if you'd been following the story, instead of romancing my secretary, *we* would've been first with this, instead of playing catch up."

Brad set his mouth as if he was preparing a reply, but Delores didn't give him time to deliver it. "You and this other guy were both there at the girl's house, on the same day, weren't you?" she demanded.

"That's right."

"Perfect. I want you to go back out and re-establish contact with the Amish girl. Let her think you'll testify on her behalf at the trial. It'll make her more likely to talk to you. I want an exclusive for the *Ledger*."

Strong, conflicting emotions swirled in Brad's chest, but he smashed them down. Delores, of all people, must never suspect that he had *feelings*.

He put on a cynical expression and raised his brows incredulously. "You *do* remember that the last time I was out there, her father ripped the *door* off my truck?"

"It was the *Ledger's* truck, and I could hardly forget," Delores replied dryly. "But you could be really useful to that girl right now if you testify. It might persuade her to talk to you. Anyway, I want you back out there tomorrow morning, bright and early."

Brad pulled his hands over his face and sighed heavily. Delores smirked and added: "Tell Sheila she'll just have to live without you for a week or two."

On that depressing note, she turned and left.

Brad sat there, with his hands over his face, for at least five minutes after. The thought of going back to Lancaster County was not a welcome one, and not even primarily because he might be murdered there.

He'd never *expected* to go back. He'd never expected to even *see* the Duchess again. In fact, he'd arranged his life around his deep belief that he would never, *ever* see her again.

Going back now would be messy. Very, *very* messy.

In the first place, Sheila would be upset because he'd be going away for two weeks at least, and she wouldn't be able to go with him.

Although, if he was really honest with himself, some *alone* time might be kind of refreshing. Sheila was high maintenance.

But as for trip itself – he was in trouble. The thought of going back to Lancaster County, of facing the Duchess again after the way they had parted, and everything that had happened since –

Messy. Unpleasant. Uber challenging. He was going to have to be at the very top of his game if he hoped to get Jemima King to talk to him again. Because after everything that had happened -- she probably *hated* him.

Any return there was fraught with danger. Her father, who beyond all doubt wanted to kill him. That boyfriend of hers, or maybe more than one, who'd probably want to fight him. But most of all, above everything – *the Duchess herself.* She had almost *supernatural* power. Power to make him destroy himself. Power to make him do crazy things, things he'd never *dream* of doing in cold blood.

Without even trying. Without even knowing that she was doing it.

He shuddered. That that was the really scary part. She was unconsciously hypnotic, like a force of nature. Like one of those sirens from Greek mythology.

All she had to do was *look* at him.

He groaned and pulled his hands over his face. Facing her again was going to be like leaning over the edge of a cliff, and praying that the wind didn't blow.

But so far, right up to that very hour, his luck with the Duchess had been nothing but bad.

Brad opened the door to O'Malley's Restaurant and strolled into the lobby. He and Sheila had gotten into the habit of having dinner there together after work. He noticed that Sheila was already there, in their usual booth. He braced himself, because when she found out he was leaving it wasn't going to be a happy evening.

She scooted over to let him slide into the seat. "Want a bite of my appetizer?" she asked, holding up a nacho.

"*Please.*"

She handed it to him, and he took a bite. Sheila snuggled in close and gave him a peck on the cheek.

"How was work today? You must've been busy because you stayed holed up in your office. You didn't even *call* me."

He turned his eyes to her smiling face. He might as well get it over with.

"Ah – about that, Sheila. Delores has decided to send me back out to the boonies for a follow up to the Washington letter story. I'll be gone for a couple of weeks, starting tomorrow."

Sheila pulled back. Her voice sounded stung. "A couple of *weeks*? What am I supposed to do in town all alone?"

Brad took a deep breath and switched his face to its *reassurance* setting. "I know, Sheila, but it won't be *too* long. Can't say no to my boss, after all," he shrugged, smiling. "I have to eat."

She straightened suddenly. "Delores could send me, too!"

"Oh, well now, I wish that were possible," he chuckled, "but Delores might have something to say about that. You're her right arm."

"No, I could ask her!" Sheila countered. Her eyes had taken on the determined look that told him she was already planning their agenda.

"Ah, *hah* now Sheila, I'd just love to have you work the story with me, but it isn't going to work out this time. It's a work trip, not play. We'll do something when I get back, I promise."

Sheila snapped back to the present with shocking suddenness. She pinched her cheek, and then slapped it smartly.

"Don't *patronize* me, you scheming rodent," she said sweetly, and the conversation ended abruptly.

That night, Brad lay awake in bed, staring at the ceiling. He was thinking that he should probably lie to Sheila about which hotel he was using because he was *really* looking forward to a little solitude.

He bit his lip. Sheila was on the high side of average in his young experience: pretty, fairly smart, self-interested, and hunting for a husband, though she knew better than to admit it. He'd grown fond of her because they were *alike*.

He considered himself the high side of average, too. He was good looking, fairly smart, self-interested, and absolutely *not* planning on marriage, though he, too, knew better than to admit it.

They suited one another. They got along, they liked one another, and neither of them was fooled by the other's nonsense. In short – they had a pleasant, mutually beneficial understanding.

He found that he really didn't want to do anything to mess that up.

He reached over to the nightstand, shook a cigarette out of the pack, and lit one up. He lay there, blowing gentle spouts of smoke toward the ceiling, until well past midnight.

CHAPTER NINE

To Brad's relief, his success with Jemima's story, and his improved status inspired Delores to spring for slightly more upscale accommodations than Uncle Bob's Amish Motel.

So at 9 a.m. the next morning, Brad was able to pull the company truck into the parking lot of the Lazy Daze Hotel and Dairy Bar just outside Serenity. It looked like a refurbished chain hotel, because unlike Uncle Bob's, it boasted a pool with a diving board, a sit down restaurant that served three meals a day, and a small store that sold a wide variety of "wholesome, organic Amish-made dairy products."

The teenage boy at the desk gave him a room on the second floor, overlooking the pool, and Brad made the weary trudge up a flight of flimsy metal steps. But when he opened the door to his room, he was rewarded with a blast of arctic air, and that indefinable *clean hotel* aroma that was equal parts guest soap, *very* faded cigarette smoke and refrigeration.

Brad dumped his gear on the big bed and collapsed face down across it. He lay there for a long while, recovering from his far too early morning.

As he lay there, he began to game out several possible scenarios by which to approach the Duchess. None of them were especially promising, but Delores had given him no choice. He told himself that forethought *now*, might preserve his teeth *later*. So --

Scenario Number One: He would drive up to the King's front door in the company truck in broad daylight, walk up the steps like a civilized man, knock on the front door, and pray that he got the woman of the house. If so, he'd fall on his knees and beg her with tears in his eyes, to *let him talk to Jemima*.

If he got the red giant -- he'd jump into the truck and gun it for parts unknown.

Scenario Number Two. He would park on the edge of the adjoining property, like before, hike across an acre of brambles, jump the fence, and hide in the bushes at the edge of the garden until Jemima came outside.

If she came outside.

Scenario Number Three. He would approach some sympathetic intermediary and beg or bribe them to contact Jemima and make his case *for* him. This seemed like the best option available, except that he didn't know anybody in Serenity who also knew Jemima, except for that sadistic geezer at the store who'd sent him on a snipe hunt.

Scenario Number Four. He would mail Jemima a letter, and beg her to meet him. And hope that she: got the letter; got it in time; didn't ignore it; didn't show it to anyone else; or send someone else, like her *father*, to the proposed meeting.

Scenario Number Five. He would call the number she gave him once and hope that somebody happened to be inside while the phone was ringing and that they cared enough to answer the call.

He beat his head against the pillow.

After a while, having failed to think of anything cleverer, he got up and stored his things, turned on the TV, and raided the mini bar. He pulled out a soda, cracked it open, and took a long pull.

The TV was playing the local news. All-too-familiar stuff – he'd covered it all – a county fair, a proposed stoplight to prevent collisions with buggies, a new business opening.

His cell phone buzzed, and when he looked down, it was Sheila. His mouth twisted into a sly grin. She had found out that he'd lied about his hotel, and that he'd turned off the geolocator, so now she was calling to figure out where he really was. And, it wasn't going to work, but it would be fun to play with her.

"Hello?"

"Hi, Brad. I was just calling to see that you got there okay."

"That was thoughtful. I'm sitting here with a tall cold one, watching TV."

"Where are you?"

He bit his lip. "Oh, I had to find another hotel besides Uncle Bob's. Some mix up with the credit card. I'm going to give Delores grief when I get back."

"Oh, how irritating. So where did you have to go?"

I'm at the Happy Acres Hotel in Marietta."

"Do you miss me?"

He rolled his eyes to the ceiling. The faint tapping sound in the background was Sheila, doing a quick Internet search, but she would soon discover that the Happy Acres Hotel, true to its Amish neighborhood, did *not* have a website.

"Sure do."

And…cue the cursing, in three…two…one….

A faint grumbling was just audible on the other end of the

line, and Brad grinned.

"Look cupcake, I have to go. Delores is calling me."

"But –"

"I'll be thinking of you."

And *click*.

He laughed to himself and pulled at the soda again. Sheila would check his story with Delores tomorrow, but he had already bought Delores' silence. Which meant that he was golden -- at least for the next few weeks.

He stretched out. It felt oddly luxurious to be alone for a few days, or at least without Sheila. Fond as he was of her, he had to admit that it was a relief to take a vacation from the games they played.

He let his eyes drift back to the TV. The news was still on. It was a story about quilting. He laughed and pulled the restaurant menu off the bedside table.

But when he looked back up again, the picture had changed. There was a distinguished older man talking to a reporter. He looked directly into the camera, smiled, and gestured elegantly with one hand.

The caption beneath him read, *Barfield Hutchinson, lawyer for Jemima King.*

Brad grabbed the remote and turned up the volume.

"...of course, being Amish, my client was reluctant to enter into a dispute such as this, but she sees it as an opportunity to vindicate herself from the accusations brought against her."

"Is it true that Miss King has given away more than $500,000?"

The lawyer smiled and shrugged gracefully. "It *is* true that my client has donated more than half of her windfall, *already*, to friends in need. True to her faith, she has spent her money helping others. She is an inspiration."

Brad felt his mouth dropping open. *Five hundred thousand dollars?*

He shook his head. If it'd been *anyone* else, he wouldn't have believed it. But having met the Duchess, he could buy it. She was crazy that way. Even from the beginning, she'd shown no interest in the money. It would be just like her to give it *all* away.

An unseen reporter stuck a mic in the lawyer's face, and the big, bright Channel 1 logo was clearly visible. Brad shook his head, cursing. Channel 1 -- that meant that *Wellman* had arrived -- and that he'd hit the ground running.

Brad was hoping he'd be able to get out ahead of the sharks, but apparently, no such luck. Now his job was exponentially harder. And, with pros like Wellman on the story, it meant that it was open season on Jemima King –

again.

He set his jaw. There was something about the Duchess that made him want to protect her from guys like Wellman. It was none of his business really, and if he tried, he'd probably get his chops busted for his pains.

But even so.

He took another sip of his drink and rolled his eyes up at the screen. Barfield Hutchinson was looking directly into the camera.

"Mr. Morton claims that my client promised to sell the letter to him, and then reneged on her promise. I'm hoping that if anyone witnessed their conversation, that he or she will *come forward.*"

Then he smiled again, with all his teeth.

CHAPTER TEN

The next morning, Brad forced himself to rise *obscenely* early – it was hardly 7 o'clock – and beat it out to the overgrown tract of land that adjoined the King farm. To his relief, no one else was there, so he parked the truck and hoofed it across the field of prickly vines to the property line.

He had spent the previous day calling Jemima's number, since it was a low-risk strategy, but as he had feared, they weren't answering their phone. So now it was on to the next scenario – the one that seemed at least plausible, since it had worked before.

Brad skirted the garden, taking care to keep out of sight behind the bushes. He peered out, and his heart jumped up into his throat. There was a young woman in the garden. Her face was turned away from him, but it had to be –

She turned her head, and his shoulders sagged. *It wasn't Jemima.* It was a plump, sharp-faced preteen with sandy brown hair and freckles. She was picking onions and putting them in a basket.

He bit his lip and cursed silently. As long as she was there, he couldn't get hold of the Duchess.

The girl worked her way closer to the edge of the garden, but never glanced his way. Brad looked closely at her. She was as ordinary as the Duchess was dazzling, but there was something about her – the way she moved, maybe – that suggested she might be a kid sister.

He was trying to decide whether or not to enlist her help when the girl settled the matter for him. Without turning her head, she said, just loudly enough:

"I see you standing there. What do you want?"

Brad's mouth dropped open. *Why, the sneaky little…*he straightened and looked around before answering: "I want to talk to Jemima."

There was a sputtering sound that might have been laughter. "You and everybody *else* in the world. What's it worth to you?"

He cocked his head to one side. "*What?*"

"You heard me. What's it worth to you? You won't get her without my help, I promise. The driveway is barricaded, and all I have to do is call my father, and you're busted."

Brad glared at her, torn between surprise, and the urge to laugh. He fished in his pocket. "I don't carry much *money*," he told her.

She shrugged, and made as if to walk away.

"Wait, *wait*!" he hissed and dug in his wallet. "How about a twenty?"

"You've got to be kidding me," she replied dryly.

He shot her an impatient glance and dug deeper. "Okay, a *fifty*. But it's all I've got."

She pretended to drop the basket and to retrieve the onions rolling across the lawn. He stuck the fifty out just far enough for her to grab, and she took it. She put it in the basket, and covered it with vegetables.

She turned her head slightly. "Wait here. I'll send her out to you." Then she made her way back to the house – slowly, and with many leisurely detours. She walked up onto the porch, and disappeared inside.

Time passed. Brad stood sweating in the bushes, craning his head for any sign of life at the front door. There was nothing.

He cursed under his breath. He was beginning to think that

the girl had played him when the screen door squeaked open, and someone stepped outside. He couldn't see who it was.

His heart began to pound, and he cursed again. Even after all these months, the Duchess did crazy things to his pulse, but he couldn't let her, not this time. He had to be at the top of his game. He made himself look down at the ground and tried to clear his mind.

When he looked up again, Jemima was walking out to the garden, her coppery hair framed by the new light shining through the trees. She was backlit by the morning sun, with a network of shining strands floating around her head like a red halo. Her eyes were that vivid, unearthly green, and her delicate profile was dreamy and soft.

She knelt down in the garden and dug in the soft earth with her small white fingers. He watched her, fascinated. She was like a Flemish painting come to life somehow, a...

He shook his head. It was happening *again*. But he wasn't going to let it throw him.

He shot a quick glance toward the house, saw no one, and took a deep breath. It was *now or never*.

He moved toward her quickly, hoping to close the distance before she noticed him. And it worked: he was at her elbow before she looked up. But when she did, his plan went south -- disastrously.

For a split second, she stared at him as if she couldn't

believe her eyes. And then her green eyes blazed.

"*You!*" she gasped. "How do you *dare* to show your face to me again, after all you've done to *me*, and to my *family*!" She put her hands on the ground and pushed up to her feet, and squared off against him, hands on hips.

"I haven't had a *moment's* peace since I sold that hateful letter! I've been hunted like a rabbit, I have no privacy even in my own *home*! All because of you, and your – your *lust for fame*!" Her angry eyes impaled him. "You *used* me, Brad Williams, and I – I –"

He tilted his head apologetically to one side. "I'm sorry it turned out the way it did, *truly*, Duchess," he told her, and oddly enough – he meant it. "But I wasn't the one who hounded you, was I? Is it fair to blame *me*, for what other people did?"

She turned and began to walk back toward the house. "You and your slick words! But I won't listen to them anymore! You are a *liar*, and you *used* me, and you've *hurt my family*, and *stolen our peace*! You're an evil, *crafty* man!"

He moved to follow. "Listen to me, Jemima! I'm here to *help* you. I saw your lawyer on the TV yesterday, he was asking for witnesses to come forward, and –"

She whirled to face him. "Leave me alone! Leave, and *never* come back! How plain do I have to make it? Go away!"

She turned again, and he grabbed her shoulders in

desperation. "Listen to me Duchess," he said urgently, looking down into her face. "I can testify at your trial. *I can help –*"

But she twisted in his arms, turned her face away from him, and cried out in frustrated German.

The next thing he knew, two big hands twisted him around. He had a split-second glimpse of some black-haired guy, and then, *fist city*.

Weren't the Amish supposed to be pacifists?

Brad went sprawling into the cabbage bed, rolled, scrambled up, and lobbed a haymaker at the stranger's jaw, sending the guy flying back into the dirt.

Brad's fist throbbed, but fear and adrenaline kept him from focusing too hard on the pain.

"*Oh halt es, bitte*," Jemima sobbed, clawing at his shoulder. He stopped long enough to look back at her, and saw that her eyes were now on the house. He followed the direction of her gaze.

Oh, no.

Brad backed away as he caught sight of the red giant – Jemina's father -- and turned to run. Jemima screamed something in German, but her father kept coming. Brad didn't want to count on this man's pacifistic tendencies, not after how the other Amish man had slugged him. Instead, Brad vaulted through the underbrush, and when the fence loomed up in front of him, jumped it like a race horse.

He plowed through the brambles as hard as he could go, scrambled down the bank to his truck, flung open the door, and jammed the keys into the ignition. The engine roared to life, and he gunned the motor.

There was suddenly a shattering *crack*, and when Brad looked into the mirror, the rear window had a hole in it.

And even more unsettling: there on the passenger seat was a rock the size of a baseball.

CHAPTER ELEVEN

That evening, Brad Williams stretched out full length on the bed in Room 321 with a glass of water in one hand, and an ice pack in the other.

He pressed the ice to his swollen jaw, swirled the water between his teeth, and closed his eyes. To judge by the way his jaw was throbbing, he was sure that he was now the proud owner of a hairline fracture. He hoped with all his heart that the other guy had at *least* a broken tooth.

Although, to be fair, that guy had probably been one of the Duchess' slaves and had just been trying to protect her.

He inhaled sharply, and closed his eyes against a new wave

of pain.

His cell phone buzzed suddenly, and he would've ignored it, but the name on the display read *Delores Watkins*. He cursed but pressed the phone gingerly to his good ear.

"Hello?"

Delores' musky voice rumbled through the speaker. "Hello, wonder boy. How's life in the green hill country?"

"*Great,*" he mumbled sardonically.

"How's your story coming?"

"Here's my headline for today," he mumbled. "*Amish People Hate Us.*"

"That's cute," Delores commiserated. "Meanwhile, did you notice that Channel 1 snagged an interview with the girl's lawyer?"

"I saw."

"Is that all you can say?"

Brad inhaled again. "For the moment."

"What's wrong with your voice? You sound like you've got cotton in your mouth."

"I got slugged."

"*Hmmm.*" Delores' voice sounded strangely unsurprised. "Well, be sure to ice it down tonight, because I don't want you looking like a piece of beef tomorrow. You're the face of the paper right now."

"You're all heart, Delores."

The other shoe suddenly dropped. Brad could practically see the light dawning on the other end of the line. "-- *Tell* me the truck is still in one piece, Brad!"

Brad groaned and hissed: "*Sssss* --- the pain! I have to go, Delores – can't talk anymore!"

He pressed a button, tossed the cell phone weakly onto the bed, and took another careful sip.

The cold drink made him suck in air, and grimace. Every muscle in his body ached, and his jaw throbbed. He was as muscular as the next guy, in fact he'd been told that he had a very nice body. He'd had *plenty of* energy last year in high school. He was something of an athlete; he'd pitched on the baseball team, he'd dated a bevy of girls, he'd hardly slept.

But something about this business today had drained him. Maybe it was the excitement of seeing the Duchess close up – as goofy as that sounded – and the adrenalin rush of a near-death experience.

But no matter where it came from, the charge he'd been running on was wearing off. He had to admit to himself that he was *exhausted*.

That dark-haired guy had nailed him with a dead-on shot to

the chops. His ears were still ringing. Even the arm he'd used to block the second shot ached.

Of course, blasting across more than an acre of brambles, at top speed, with the Duchess' father right at his heels had cost him a little something, too. He felt as if he could sleep for a week.

He closed his eyes, and tried to relax. His hotel room was quiet, and thankfully, he had no near neighbors. The only sound he could hear was the faint chirp of birds outside, calling to each other as the light faded.

Gradually, the pain in his jaw receded enough for him to drift off into a twilight sleep. The Duchess was in his arms again, but this time, she wasn't impatient, and didn't try to pull away. The sound of her dulcet voice whispered in his ear. She was still angry, she was still telling him to beat it, but she was doing it in such a soft voice that even "get lost" sounded hot.

He dozed for a few hours, and when he woke up again, it was early evening. The sky outside was dim, and lights shimmered over the blue pool water.

He sighed and stretched. He couldn't remember what he had dreamed, if he had dreamed anything, but for some strange reason -- he woke up thinking about what happened to you, when you died.

For the first time in his life, he wondered if he really might

-- as several people had suggested – *be headed to hell*.

He remembered the Duchess' angry eyes, and hoped devoutly that the decision wasn't up to *her*. He reached for the glass on the bedside table, and took another sip.

He'd never really given an afterlife any serious consideration, and probably wouldn't have now, except that he was in Amish country, where they thought about that sort of thing all the time. Plus, he had almost been murdered that afternoon, and it was sort of a reminder that he could, well -- actually *die*.

The thought was creepy, and he shook it off, but it was persistent.

What would happen to him, if he died?

Nothing, probably – he'd just cease to exist. Or at least, he'd always assumed that was true. Neither of his parents had made any mention of what they thought on the subject, and since they'd *both* been deadbeats, he wouldn't have paid attention if they had. Brad took another careful sip of his water.

His friends at school hadn't talked about it, either. He'd assumed that they were agnostics, like he was himself; at any rate, they lived as if they didn't believe in any God. Even the religious kids at school had been pretty much like everyone else -- no important difference that he'd noticed.

Jemima was the only person he'd ever known who acted

like she really believed all that religious stuff. She was the only person he'd even *heard* of who would give away half a million dollars of her own money, without spending a dime of it on herself.

That was pretty crazy, when he thought about it. But also – he had to admit it – pretty *amazing*, too.

Of course, Jemima hated him right now, and maybe she had a right to hate him. In his own defense, he really *had* believed that getting rich would be great for her, but maybe it hadn't been so great after all – at least for an Amish girl, who wasn't into *things*. Maybe it had just complicated her life.

And maybe she was even right about his motives. Maybe he *had* used her, a little, to get a job at the paper. Another pain hit him suddenly. It was sharp, and deep, but this pain wasn't in his jaw. It felt like it was somewhere under his ribcage, somewhere too deep to soothe with an ice pack.

Jemima had accused him of lying, and using her, and not caring about what she thought, or wanted, or even needed. She had called him everything except a child of God.

He twisted his lip. Maybe she was right. Maybe he *wasn't* one.

He glanced over at the bedside table. He'd noticed that someone had stuck a Bible in the top drawer, and he reached out and opened it.

It was a plain brown book. It looked inexpensive, and it

was written in some impenetrable medieval dialect.

But he opened it anyway. He'd heard of it all his life, but had never cracked it open before.

He flipped through it idly, and stopped at a random point near the front. The text read:

"And the LORD said unto me, Say unto them. Go not up, neither fight; for I am not among you; lest ye be smitten before your enemies.

"So I spake unto you; and ye would not hear, but rebelled against the commandment of the LORD, and went presumptuously up into the hill.

"And the Amorites, which dwelt in that mountain, came out against you, and chased you, as bees do, and destroyed you in Seir, even unto Hormah."

Brad pinched his lips into a straight line, looked up at the ceiling, and hurriedly flipped the book closed again, as if he'd been stung.

CHAPTER TWELVE

The next morning, Brad stared at his face in the hotel room mirror. The swelling had gone down to the point that his jaw looked almost normal, but now he had the *mother* of all bruises.

He tilted his head, studying it. It was going to be a *beauty*. It was roughly the size and shape of an apple – or a *fist* – and was already a dusky purple, shading to black at the point of impact, just below his lower lip.

The only way that he could hope to hide it was with massive amounts of face makeup, but there were some things he refused to do, even for his career. He didn't care if some other male reporters did it, and he didn't care if Delores *fired* him -- he wasn't going out with *makeup* on his face, like a girl.

He sighed and splashed his face with cold water, and dried it off.

Since his attempt to contact the Duchess at her home had blown up, and had almost resulted in his murder, now he had to fall back on the only other viable alternative he had left – trying to reach her through somebody else. And luckily for him – now he had a *prospect*.

Approximately 20 minutes later, Brad parked the truck outside the office of Barfield Hutchison, attorney at law. The prim brick two-story was standard issue lawyer digs: an upscale mansion from 100 years ago, suggestive of wealth and success. Brad glanced at his jaw in the rearview mirror and grimaced, but got out of the truck and entered boldly, nevertheless.

The fetching brunette sitting at the desk inside swept him with her long lashes. Her smile communicated approval, more than a bit of speculation, and even – if he wasn't mistaken – a certain amount of interest. "Good morning," she purred. "*May I help you?*"

Brad gave her his card. "I'm Brad Williams from the *Ledger* Newspaper. I was hoping to talk to Mr. Hutchinson about the Jemima King case."

The semi-flirtatious look vanished from the woman's face.

Her smile froze for an instant. She shifted her weight, cleared her throat, recalibrated, and smiled again. "I'll check. Please sit down, Mr. Williams."

Brad nodded his thanks, and settled into a leather chair a few feet away from the secretary's desk. He crossed his legs and tried to look patient and professional, but his pulse was thrumming in his neck. This was crunch time. If Hutchinson refused to play ball, he was out of luck, because the old shark was his last chance to get in touch with Jemima.

But to his relief, Barfield Hutchinson seemed perfectly willing to *play ball*.

The secretary's phone rang, and she murmured into it briefly and hung up. She looked up at him and smiled again. "Mr. Hutchinson will see you now," she informed him.

When he entered the lawyer's office, the older man was sitting behind a massive antique desk and was reading documents through horn-rimmed spectacles -- the very picture of a prosperous small town lawyer.

Hutchinson looked up at him and nodded toward a chair. "Well, well, good morning, Mr. Williams! I don't need to ask who *you* are and what you do – the whole country knows your name! Please sit down."

Brad sank into a leather chair and looked into Hutchinson's face. He didn't have time to beat around the bush.

"I know that Miss King is being sued for a lot of money,"

he said, without preamble. "I've come here to make you an offer."

The older man looked up, smiled, and raised his snowy brows. "I see," he said gently. "And what sort of *offer* are you making me, Mr. Williams?"

"I was there when Caldwell Morton talked to Jemima King about the antique clock," Brad told him. "And I'm willing to testify in court that she did *not* promise to sell it to him. I can also testify that he tried to bully her into selling it to him, and that it didn't work."

Mr. Hutchinson nodded, but his blue eyes were very bright and sharp. "I'm assuming there's a condition?"

Brad returned his smile. "There's a condition. I want to be able to talk to Miss King again, alone. I want to talk to her here, in your office."

The older man frowned faintly. "I'm not sure I follow you, Mr. Williams. You do realize that I can just subpoena you?"

Brad set his jaw. "If you do, you'll get nothing from me."

"What do you want to talk to my client about?"

Brad felt himself going hot, but he stared the older man down. "I want another interview," he replied evenly.

"Well, I'm sure you know that I can't promise that my client will agree to your conditions, Mr. Williams. Have you" – his eye fell on Brad's jaw – "talked to Miss King *yourself*?"

Brad struggled to keep his tone even. "I can't talk to Miss King at her own home for various reasons," he replied. "I won't bore you with them now. But I'd like to talk to her here, at your office, alone, for just a few minutes. If I can just do that -- I'll testify."

Hutchinson's expression was an unspoken comment. He shrugged slightly. "I'll pass your offer along to my client, Mr. Williams," he sighed, "but I can't make any promises. It's a very unusual request. *So* unusual, in fact, that I don't mind telling you that I'm tempted to advise her against it."

Brad pinched his lips together and leaned across the desk. "Just so long as you *give her the message*. Here's my card. I'm staying at a hotel in town. She can call me at this number, day or night."

The older man took the card, smiled thinly, and nodded. "I'll make sure she gets it, Mr. Williams."

Brad rose and turned for the door, but before he had reached it, the older man added smoothly:

"You'll forgive me, Mr. Williams, but no one can fail to notice that my client is a remarkably lovely young woman. For years, lovely young women were the reason for most of the lawsuits I saw. And they are routinely – you could almost say, *monotonously* -- the downfall of ambitious young men."

Brad swallowed the reply he wanted to make, flung open the door, and slapped it closed behind him with more force than was strictly necessary -- or politic.

CHAPTER THIRTEEN

Jemima King lay full length on her bed with her face crammed into her pillow. The only light in her dark bedroom was a narrow yellow bar underneath the door.

There was a soft knock, and Jemima lifted her face.

"Who is it?"

"*Mamm.*"

Jemima hurriedly wiped her eyes. "Come in," she murmured.

The door opened slowly and her mother appeared in it,

framed in light. She crossed the distance between them and sat quickly on the bed.

She held out her arms wordlessly and Jemima went into them, sobbing.

"There, now," her mother smiled, caressing her hair. "It's been a hard day, I know."

"Oh, Mamm, why does everything I do go so bad *wrong*?" Jemima cried. "I'm being sued for money I don't have, and the reporter is *back*, and now Mark has done what he shouldn't, and gotten hurt -- and it's all my fault!"

Her mother made a soft *hush* sound. "*None* of those things are your fault," Rachel soothed. "They're not your fault -- my poor girl. You will understand that better when you're not so upset." She kissed Jemima's cheek and smiled. "And everything is going to be all right."

Jemima shook her head. "I don't see *how*. I wish I could go back and – and *undo* everything I've done this summer!"

Her mother took her hand. "See now -- the Englischer sued you because he chose *money* over telling the truth. That young reporter is back because he wants another story. And Mark is hurt because he did what he should *not* have done. He lost his temper, and forgot who he is, and struck another human being with his fist. Mark is the one who will have to repent of that, my Mima. Not *you*."

"But he did it because of me," Jemima whispered.

"That may be," her mother replied, "but you didn't tell him to do it."

"No," Jemima shuddered. "It was *awful*! They were hitting each other and fighting like wild animals! But even that wasn't the worst," Jemima sobbed. "*Daed* chased Brad Williams all the way to the fence, and over the fence, and across the field next door, and – and I think he would have *hit* him, if he'd caught him!" She broke down into fresh tears, and her mother looked up at the ceiling.

"Your father –" she paused, coughed, and began again – "your father *also* did what he should not have done. He lost his temper, *too*, and forgot who he is." She looked down at her daughter's face tenderly. "When you have a daughter of your own, my Mima, you will understand better."

Jemima grew quiet in her mother's arms. "I forgot, too, Mamm," she whispered. "I was *upset* with Daed, for treating Brad Williams with such anger. But, I was angry with Brad Williams myself, and I said mean, hateful things to him. I called him a liar, and a user, and said he was *evil,* and it wasn't even the first time! Then I – I told him to go away, and never come back!"

She broke down into tears again. "But he said he wanted to *help* me. He makes me so angry sometimes, that I *forget* how much he's done for me. That he gave up a million dollars -- so I could have it!"

Rachel's face grew grim. "I think that young man helps

himself first, Mima," she replied carefully. "He's here because he wants a story for his paper. He told you that -- didn't he?"

Jemima stared over her mother's shoulder and said nothing.

"I know that you're on your rumspringa, Mima," her mother said gently, "but just because you're free to do what you please, doesn't mean that you're free of the consequences that will come from what you choose. I don't know what you feel toward that boy, Mima, if you feel anything. But I do know this: That boy is an Englischer. He lives in a different world. He thinks differently from you, he *believes* different things, and he *wants* different things. If you lose sight of that, you could be very bad hurt."

She smoothed Jemima's rumpled hair back from her brow. "That's what we worry about, your father and I. We want you to be happy, Mima. But more than that, we want you to be useful, and good, and right with God. The man you choose can help you be all those things.

"Or hinder you."

Jemima said nothing and kept her face buried in her mother's shoulder. Rachel kissed her again and then patted her shoulder.

"Come downstairs, and talk to your father. You owe him an apology, too, you know, after the things you said to him."

Jemima nodded wordlessly.

"I was *surprised*, Jemima, I have to say," her mother chided gently. "I've never heard you talk to your father in such a tone before. He loves you very much, but you've hurt him with your thoughtless words."

Jemima fought back tears. "I'm sorry, Mamm," she whispered. "It's just that – I was scared what could have happened if Daed had caught Brad Williams. Would he have hit him, like Mark? It frightened me, and it made me angry, too. Daed should ask me before he – before he – just decides!"

"Your father doesn't trust reporters," Rachel answered, "and he's wise. Most of them have been nothing but trouble to us. That boy was trespassing, and not for the first time. When your father arrived, he was fighting Mark! He's behaved very strangely all along, Mima. Your father was right to chase that boy away -- he's only trying to protect you."

Jemima fell silent, and her mother took her hand. "Come downstairs now, Mima. You have something important to say to your father."

Her mother put an arm around her waist, and Jemima allowed herself to be led out and downstairs. Her mother accompanied her to the door of her father's study but left her at the door.

Jemima looked after her wistfully, but turned the knob and went in.

Her father was sitting in the big red chair. He was leaning forward, with his elbows resting on his knees, but he looked up as she entered.

It only needed one glance at his wounded expression to make Jemima break down.

"I'm *sorry*, Daed," she whimpered.

Her father stood quickly and opened his arms. Jemima ran into them.

"I'm *sorry* I said such mean things to you," she cried. "I didn't mean them. I was just – scared that you were going to *hit* Brad Williams -- like Mark!"

Jacob closed his big arms around his daughter and smiled his forgiveness, but his eyes remained troubled. "I lost my temper, it's true," he told her. "That was wrong of me, and I'll have to repent -- again." He paused, and a dissatisfied expression flitted briefly across his face.

He returned to his daughter. "But that makes no difference for *you*. It isn't right for you to *disrespect your father*, Jemima King," he added firmly, looking her in the eyes. "You did wrong, and you'll have to be punished for it. Your mother and I, we've – we've decided that you will not attend any Sings or frolics for two weeks. It will give you a chance to think about your behavior."

Jemima nodded, and hugged him. "All right, Daed," she murmured.

Jacob relaxed visibly, as if he'd been worried. He tightened his arms around his daughter, and closed his eyes.

"Now run off to bed," he told her. "Morning comes early, and you've had a hard day."

Jemima smiled, and kissed him, and slipped out; and after she had gone, Rachel appeared in the doorway, entered, and closed the door after her.

"How did it go?" she asked softly.

Jacob frowned. "She apologized, and I know she meant it."

Rachel smiled. "I knew she would. She adores you, Jacob."

Jacob did not seem comforted. "I was never worried about that part." He frowned, and bit his thumbnail.

Rachel looked a question. "Why, are you worried about something else?"

Jacob looked up at his pretty wife. "Yes. I'm worried that she cried about that Englischer boy *all day*, but only asked once about Mark!"

CHAPTER FOURTEEN

It was now early fall. The sky was bright blue without clouds, and the air had turned crisp and cool in the morning. The hills around the King farm were spattered with pale greens, and golds, and blush pinks that would deepen to reds. Every field was full of corn, or wheat, and the trees were heavy with fruit. It was harvest time, and the sounds of harvest wafted faintly across the valley every afternoon.

Jacob King was a blacksmith, not a farmer, but he, too, was busy. He had returned to his smithy, and the sound of his hammer joined the other sounds in the valley the next morning, as Jemima began her day.

Jemima found some comfort in the rhythm of daily work.

She washed clothes, and hung them out to dry on the line. Then she spent the afternoon helping her mother put up vegetables, fruit, jam, soup, and sauces against the approach of winter. Rachel's root cellar would soon be packed, with row on row of shining glass jars filled with good things to eat.

At mid-afternoon, they took a break. Rachel and Jemima went to sit in the swing on the front porch, and rock, and drink iced tea for a few minutes before finishing up the last batch of creamed corn. Jemima sank gratefully onto the swing, and took a long drink, and sighed. A cool breeze moved the air, and she closed her eyes. After hours of kitchen work, it felt *good.*

Deborah walked up the steps as they sat there and tossed the day's mail down into Jemima's lap. Rachel fixed her with a kindling eye.

"Where have you been all morning, Deborah?" she asked. "I needed you to help us with the canning!"

Deborah shrugged, and Jemima looked down at her feet. She foresaw another whipping in her sister's future.

"Oh, Sarah Lapp asked me to come over to her house today," she replied lightly.

Her mother pinched her lips into a straight line. "Well, never mind. But make yourself useful now! Your sister has done both her work and *yours,* all morning. So you can take over from now on. Go upstairs and get washed up."

"But –"

Rachel answered with unusual firmness. "Do as I say!" she cried, and Deborah was so surprised at this rebuke, that she closed her mouth and actually *obeyed*.

Rachel set her glass down on the porch and gave Jemima a rueful glance. "And you, Jemima, you may do as you please this afternoon, because you helped me this morning."

Then she set her mouth, and followed her errant youngest daughter inside.

Jemima watched them go, sighed, and turned to the sheaf of mail on her lap. Most of the letters were for her father, but two of them were addressed to her.

Jemima smiled. One of them was unmistakably from Joseph. She would recognize his broad, looping handwriting anywhere.

She tore the envelope open and unfolded the letter. Its contents expressed a certain amount of agitation.

"My maus," it began, *"I was very surprised to hear Samuel Kauffman say that you told him that we were not engaged. How can that be? After our night of passion –"*

Jemima frowned in faint puzzlement. He must mean the night he came to the house, and *kissed* her so pleasantly.

"—how could we be anything but engaged? I know that you return my feelings, my sweet maus, and could never have said what Samuel claims."

Jemima closed her eyes, and put a hand on her head, because it had begun to ache. In all the turmoil, she hadn't had a chance to talk to Joseph. One *more* thing gone wrong – one more thing she would have to set right, if she could.

To Jemima's dismay, the letter continued: *"I consider you my wife already, Jemima, just as if we were standing in front of the bishop. And I have made it plain to Samuel Kauffman, and certain others, that we are engaged, and that I will not look kindly on any of them coming out to your house, or trying to court with you."*

"*Oh!*" Jemima put a hand to her mouth, closed her eyes, and shook her head. Really, sometimes Joseph Beiler was so - - *so* – she just wanted to *shake* him.

"I will be coming to see you again. I know that you depend on my strength, my maus, and I will soon be at your side."

"Oh, *Joseph!*" Jemima exclaimed, in exasperation. How on earth had he gotten *all that*, out of their last meeting? But on the other hand, how on earth could she tell him *anything*, when she wasn't sure whether she wanted to be free – or to *let* him tell the world that they were engaged?

And then there was Samuel, waiting for an answer to *his* proposal of marriage. And Mark, who'd asked her not to say *yes* to anyone, until after the trial, when he had hinted that *he'd* propose, as well!

Jemima shook her head in misery, and looked up at the sky. *Oh Lord,* she prayed, *Please help me! I'm in so far over my head, I don't know what to do!*

She sighed, and put Joseph's letter aside, making a mental note to call him later, even though she wasn't yet sure what she would *say.*

She picked up the other letter. It was heavy, and slick, and the envelope was professionally printed. It was from Barfield Hutchinson – the lawyer. It could hardly be *good* news, but Jemima made herself open it in spite of the dread she felt.

When she unfolded it, the neat, typed contents read:

"Dear Miss King:

A few days ago I received a visit at my office from a young man named Brad Williams."

Jemima's heart jumped up into her throat and throbbed there.

"Mr. Williams asked me to relay a message to you, and I agreed to do so. He says that he is willing to testify on your behalf in court, but only on the condition that you meet with him at my office, alone. I leave this completely to your own discretion. As you know, your court date is fast approaching. Mr. Williams' testimony could be very useful to us in court,

because he says he is ready to swear that he heard you tell Mr. Morton that you wouldn't sell the clock, and that Mr. Morton tried to intimidate you.

"However, should you decline Mr. Williams' offer, we will most likely still prevail. It is my opinion, based on years of experience, that Mr. Morton is bluffing, and that he is trying to bully you. He clearly believes that you will settle out of court, because of your religious tradition. But he can ill afford a jury case, and his lawyer at least will be aware of that.

"I have enclosed the card that Mr. Williams left. Should you choose to meet him here, please call my office to inform us of your decision.

"Yours sincerely,

Barfield Hutchinson, P.A."

Jemima let the letter fall out of her hands. A dozen conflicting emotions swirled up around her like birds startled from cover. They circled around her, fought, fought again, entwined, and then exploded into a burst of feeling that was almost like color, like bells.

And that vibrated deep in her heart for long afterwards.

She looked down at her lap. Just below the letter was the business card that she remembered. She picked it up, ran a small thumb over the stiff, heavy paper.

She turned her head toward the house. Kitchen sounds came through the screen door: the clink of glass jars, her mother's soothing voice, and occasionally, Deborah's sharp voice, raised in complaint.

She listened for a minute and then turned her head toward her father's smithy, next to the barn. The sound of hammering and the hiss of fire drowned in water, wafted faintly from the open door.

She looked out across the yard, and beyond it, across their meadow, further to the road, and beyond it to their neighbor's fields. There wasn't another human face in all that expanse: just the golden light of late afternoon, slanting across endless acres of corn.

Jemima turned the card in her fingers again, as if she were memorizing its texture. Then she stood, glanced at the screen door, and moved silently across the porch and down the steps.

CHAPTER FIFTEEN

Jemima got out of the cab and turned to pay the Englisch driver, who smiled, nodded, and slowly pulled the car away.

Jemima watched it disappear down the tree-lined street, and then turned to her destination. The elegant, two-story brick mansion that was the law office of Barfield Hutchinson looked just the same as it had been the last time she had seen it. It was still opulent, still a reminder of fighting and conflict, and still – *very* intimidating. She took a deep breath, shook out her skirts, and walked quickly up the cobbled driveway.

The grandfather clock in the corner was chiming when she stepped in. It was just three o'clock, and she was right on time.

The secretary looked up as she entered, and smiled politely. "Good afternoon, Miss King! You'll find Mr. Williams waiting for you in the consultation room. It's through that doorway, second room to the left."

"Thank you," Jemima nodded.

She walked across the plush carpet, noting that her feet hardly made a sound on it. The ticking of the big antique clock sounded loud in the stillness. She turned into a small hallway, and approached the second door on the left. It was closed.

Jemima paused outside of it, praying silently. Then she turned the knob and walked in.

Brad Williams was sitting at a big table, but stood as she entered. There was a big picture window behind him, and afternoon light flooded through it. His wild sandy hair seemed outlined in white light, and his light blue eyes looked almost on fire in his shadowed face.

But her eyes zoomed straight to his chin. Brad Williams' chin was still stamped with the imprint of Mark's fists. There was a horrible, purplish stain on one side of his jaw that spread all the way to his chin. In places, it looked *black*.

She gasped out loud. "*Oh! Es tut mir leid, das ist alles meine schuld...*"

He grinned a little crookedly, and lifted his hands. Jemima shook her head and reverted to English.

"Oh, your face! I'm so sorry!" she cried. She sank down into her chair and stared at him in horror.

He grinned again, and shrugged. "No worries, Duchess. I'm a big boy. It's an occupational hazard."

Jemima took a breath before she replied: "I'm *so sorry* that this happened to you. I know that Mark will be sorry too, when he has had time to think."

Brad smiled and rubbed his jaw gingerly. "Is that his name? Well, it's apt. He sure left one."

Jemima burst out into a sob, swallowed it, and put a hand to her mouth.

"Hey now," Brad objected, rising from his chair. "It's not as bad as all that, I promise! It looks pretty ugly, I admit, but it's not painful. See, I'll show you."

He came to the end of the table and knelt down beside her chair so that she was looking into his eyes. He smiled again.

"Go ahead – poke it," he told her.

Jemima stared at him in consternation, wondering briefly if he truly *was* mad. She shook her head.

"Go ahead. I promise I won't yell."

Jemima looked doubtfully into his eyes. He looked as if he was just going to *stay* there until she did, so she slowly and hesitantly extended a finger, and briefly touched his chin on the least-damaged-looking spot.

He squinched his face into a dreadful comic knot, with his eyes squeezed shut and his mouth puckered up. He looked so silly that she couldn't help feeling relieved, and sputtered out just a *tiny* laugh.

He winked at her. "That's right, Duchess. No worries." He pulled up a chair beside her and turned it so that he could face her. "So, now that we've established that I'm *not* murdered -- let me tell you why I asked you here."

He leaned forward and looked earnestly into her face. "What I was trying to say to you before, Duchess, is that I'm willing to testify on your behalf. Since I was there that day, when the guy was trying to get the clock from you. It might help you win in court."

Fresh tears dazzled her eyes. She shook her head and looked down into her lap. "I'm so *sorry*, Brad Williams," she said, "I said such mean things to you. You've been so kind *always*, you've always helped. It's true that things have been...sometimes hard since I sold the letter, but that wasn't *your* fault. You're not to blame for what other people do. I was wrong to take out all my anger on -- on *you*."

She peeped up at his face. His eyes looked solemn, and a little sad.

"Don't worry about it," he said quietly. "If anyone here is apologizing, it should be me. I should've thought more about how all this would affect your life. I made the mistake of assuming that a million dollars would be great for you. But I guess that's not what you're all about, huh?"

Jemima shook her head.

"And don't start feeling bad about me," he added, looking down. "I wanted a full time job at the *Ledger*. Your story helped me get it. That factored in, too, Duchess. I'm no victim."

She looked up at him again, and this time, she held his gaze. "That's why you did what you did?" she asked.

He bit his lip, but nodded.

She looked down into her lap, and then raised her eyes again. "Is that why you did – *everything* you did?"

He looked at her for a long moment, but finally shook his head. "*No.*"

Then he took her chin in one hand and held it perfectly still as he leaned in and kissed her. His kiss was softer than a sigh, barely tangible, and yet it electrified her in a way that she could hardly describe. Every nerve ending in her body strained toward that faint, soft contact, and every nerve registered its exquisite, *barely-thereness.*

He pulled back, released her chin, and smiled down into her eyes. "And call me *Brad*."

He reached down along her arm, in a faint caress, and

grabbed her hand, squeezed it. "Let's get out of here, Duchess. We can grab a sandwich in some drive thru and go have lunch. I know a pretty spot down by the river that has a picnic bench. *Come on.*"

He smiled at her winningly, and looked so handsome, in spite of his bruises, that she smiled back.

"Because I want to hear your life story, from the *day you were born, until now*. I want to know what you think, what you hate, what you love, and what you want. I want to know *everything* there is to know about you."

Jemima stared at him, but his expression was so gentle, and his eyes so warm, that she let him pull her to her feet and lead her away.

CHAPTER SIXTEEN

The experience of being inside a car was a rare one for Jemima. She associated it with illness, or emergencies. The idea of a *pleasant* car ride was new to her.

But that afternoon, she enjoyed riding in Brad Williams' truck as much as she'd enjoyed anything in a long time. The way he drove the truck reminded her of a hawk swooping down to catch a fish: *zoom*.

He took them through a drive thru and bought everything on the menu that she even looked at: coffee, and danish, and salad, and sandwich, and fries, and shake, and ice cream. When she protested, he'd only grinned, and told her that it was his treat.

He drove her out to a little park outside of town, and they took their improvised picnic to one of the tables overlooking the water. It was a bright, sunny afternoon, with white clouds sailing in a blue sky. The river was clear and shallow, and made a pleasant *hush* sound as it flowed over the rocks. There were a few families relaxing nearby, and children ran back and forth on the grass.

Brad Williams' light eyes met hers across the table. "So tell me your story," he said, pointing at her with a french fry. "Who is Jemima King?"

Jemima colored, and shrugged. "Nobody," she answered. "At least, nobody different from anybody else." She looked up at him. "I sew a little, I bake, I cook. Any Amish girl can do the same."

He half-smiled, and tilted his head, as if he couldn't quite believe her reply, but it had been the truth. She took a bite of her hamburger to spare herself the necessity of answering another immediate question.

"How old are you?" he asked.

She took a sip of cola. "Seventeen. Eighteen in November."

"I saw a younger girl in your yard this last time," he told her. "Was that your sister?"

Jemima nodded. "Yes, Deborah. She's my only sister. I have no brothers. My father is a blacksmith, and his father and his father's father were blacksmiths. I think he was a little disappointed that he didn't have a son, to carry on the tradition."

Brad fell silent and took a big bite of pie. Jemima realized, with a pang, that the mention of her father could hardly be pleasant for him.

"I – I'm sorry that my Daed chased you, Brad Williams," she told him, in a chastened tone.

"*Brad*," he corrected quickly. She smiled and amended, "*Brad*" – though it felt very strange to call an Englisch man by his first name.

"My father is a good, gentle man, *truly*, but there have been so many people at our home since I sold the letter. Reporters, who come out at night and shine lights on our house. And people who come to steal things from us, to sell. Some of the people have been *wahnsinnig* – crazy in the *head*!" she told him earnestly. "*They* were so many, and my father is only *one*. He – he has had a very hard time."

To her surprise, Brad's face flushed – unmistakably, with embarrassment. He shook his head. "I'm sorry, Duchess," he told her. "really. It sounds like this whole thing has been a nightmare for you, instead of the amazing thing I thought it would be. Any Englisch person would've been over the moon. But I guess that's the difference between being Englisch, and being Amish," he concluded ruefully.

Jemima ate her lunch and refrained from a reply. There was nothing she could say to soften that because it was true.

He looked up at her, sighed and smiled a white, lopsided grin. "So -- what do you do for *fun?*" he asked jokingly.

She looked up at him. "I go to sings, after Sunday night worship," she told him, "and frolics, and sometimes volleyball, or softball. But I just watch," she confided. "I'm not very good at *sports*."

He raised his bushy, woolly-worm eyebrows and smiled. Jemima colored, thinking that her life must seem unbearably dull to him – a reporter, who had seen so much, and had gone to so many places. She hurried to change the subject.

"And – what about *you?*" she asked shyly.

He gave her a lopsided smile. "Me? I'm a reporter for the *Ledger*." He seemed disinclined to say any more, and it made Jemima tilt her head.

She regarded him curiously. "Yes, but -- you have family, don't you?"

Brad went red again, and he looked out into the trees suddenly, as if the question made him uncomfortable. "Actually, no. No, I don't, at least, not any family that I care to claim." He brought his eyes back to hers. "My father left us when I was small, and my Mom – well, she did drugs. She died years ago. I lived with my grandmother for awhile, until she died. But by that time, I was a senior in high school and old enough to look out for myself. So I got a scholarship to a city college, and a part-time job at the paper."

Jemima dropped her gaze to the table for fear that they would betray the shock and horror she felt. She couldn't imagine what it would be like to have *no parents*, and to be forced out into the world *alone*. She tried to keep her voice light.

"Where do you go to church?"

He raised his brows politely, and Jemima felt herself going red. Evidently, the answer was, *nowhere*. He looked like he was stifling laughter.

"Ah – I don't. I'm not the religious type, I'm afraid. Though I have no problem with people who are," he added, with a smile. "Live and let live, that's me."

"Oh."

"Isn't that what the Amish say?"

Jemima looked up at him. "Oh, *yes*," she assured him, "live and – and *let* live."

He put his elbows on the picnic table and trained his bright eyes on her face. "Am I asking too many questions?"

Her mouth formed a small O. She shook her head. "It's just that, there's not that much to *tell*," she smiled. "I live a very quiet life."

His smile faded, but his eyed remained warm. "Have you ever thought about living a different kind of life?" he asked. "Say – going out into the world?"

Her eyes flew to his. "Oh, no! I could never leave my family, and my friends, or change what I believe!" she said earnestly. "No, I'm very happy. All I've ever wanted is –" she broke off suddenly, and looked down.

But he made her finish. "Is what?" he pressed gently.

She shrugged, and kept her eyes on the table. "What every Amish girl wants. To get married, to build a family. To live quietly, to be useful, to worship God in peace."

He watched her wistfully. "That last part is important to you, isn't it?" he asked.

She raised her brows in puzzlement. "Of *course*."

He took a drink, and coughed, and looked away. "And that guy Mark – is he a friend of yours?"

Jemima went hot, and looked down, and didn't reply. Brad smiled at her expression. "I just figured, since he objected so strongly to my visit."

Jemima pinched her lips together, and raised her eyes to his. "I have many friends," she told him evenly. "Mark is one of my oldest. I've known him since we were children."

He held her gaze. "Is he your boyfriend?"

Jemima looked at him in exasperation. He was beginning to irritate her again. She decided suddenly to push back, just a *little*.

"He's one of them," she replied calmly. "There are *three* boys who've asked to court with me."

He frowned faintly. "*Court* with you?"

Jemima repressed a smile, and told him teasingly: "It's almost like being *engaged*."

She had half-hoped for him to be dismayed, but to her surprise, he laughed outright. "You mean you're engaged to *three* guys?" he sputtered. "I'm not *surprised* you have that many guys who want to marry you, Duchess, but –"

She felt herself going hot. "No, of course I'm not engaged to them *all*!" she replied warmly, "just that they've *asked* me to be!"

He grinned at her. "Are you gonna marry one of them?" he asked.

She stared at him. He was shamelessly curious – bordering on rude. No one she knew would ever have *dreamed* of asking such a personal question. She hadn't expected it, and for an instant she was speechless. "I – I haven't decided," she sputtered.

To her amazement, he seemed *delighted* by her reply. He pressed a napkin to his mouth, leaned back, and regarded her with a wide grin. He pointed at her with a plastic fork.

"I wouldn't be afraid to bet $100 that you won't marry any of them," he announced.

"What!"

He stood up and brushed crumbs off of his lap. "That's right." He came over and sat down beside her, very close. Then he turned and looked her in the eyes.

"Because when you like someone *that* much, Duchess, you know *right away*."

Then he took her in his arms, and kissed her again, in front of God and everybody.

CHAPTER SEVENTEEN

"*There* she is!"

Jacob had been sitting at the kitchen table, but he rose and put his hands on his hips as Jemima walked in the front door. "Where have you *been* all day, young lady?" he demanded.

"Are you all right, Jemima?" Rachel added. Her anxious eyes were glued to Jemima's face. "*Look* at her, Jacob!"

Her father walked up and lifted her chin to the light. "You're right, she looks flushed." He covered her brow with one big palm. "Not running a fever, though."

Jemima lifted troubled eyes to father's face. "I feel fine," she told him.

Deborah raked her with a shrewd glance. "*Pffft*! She's been with one of her boyfriends," she scoffed and went back to her dinner.

Jacob's expression darkened. "Is that true, Jemima?" he demanded sternly.

Jemima cast her eyes down. "I went to the lawyer's office," she stammered. "He sent me a letter." She soothed her guilty conscience by telling himself *that* part was true enough.

Her parents exchanged a wordless look but seemed to accept her explanation, to her relief.

"What did the lawyer say, Mima?" her mother asked.

Jemima put her bag down and went to sit at the table. "He says he thinks my chances are good because Mr. Morton is bluffing and wants me to settle out of court," she replied. "He says that he thinks he'll *destroy* Mr. Morton if the case goes to a jury," she replied literally.

Her mother frowned her disapproval. "*That* is why we don't go to court, Jemima," she chided, "Fighting and talk of beating, of *destroying*! It isn't right to do such things!"

Jacob half-turned. "We've talked about this before, Rachel," he said quietly, and she fell silent; but not before giving him an unhappy look.

"Mr. Hutchinson says that my appearance is next week,"

Jemima continued. "He says he'll send a car to pick me up, and drive us to the courthouse. And not to be worried."

"I hope you told him that we are *not* worried, no matter the outcome," Rachel replied. "Now eat your dinner."

Jemima obeyed and said little else. She helped her mother clean up after, and joined her family for evening prayers, but once when she opened her eyes, she noticed that Deborah's sharp eyes were open, too – and watching her.

When prayers were done, they all went upstairs for the night. Jemima closed her bedroom door behind her, and changed into her nightgown, and plaited her hair. But she didn't even bother to turn down her lamp, because there was *no* chance that she would drop off to sleep, not for a long time.

She reclined on her bed and closed her eyes. In an instant, she was in Brad Williams' – *Brad*'s arms again, and his kisses were sending shivers up and down her spine. No matter how guilty it made her feel, she couldn't help reliving it. No one else had ever made her feel so – she couldn't describe it – so deliciously *burned up*.

Because somehow, Brad Williams was on fire, from his crazy eyes outward. He did insane things, like he had no fear, and maybe he was an Englischer, and maybe a madman, too, but when he kissed her, he kissed her like it was the last time, like the world was ending, like they were both going to die.

No one, not Mark, not Samuel, not even Joseph, had *ever* made her feel like Brad made her feel.

And that was a *problem*.

There was a soft knock at the door, and Jemima opened her eyes. "Come in," she called.

To her surprise, when the door opened, Deborah stood in it, braiding her long hair. She closed the door behind her, swung her braid behind her, and put her hands on her hips. "So, you like the Englisch reporter," she said, matter-of-factly. "What do you plan to do with Joseph, and Samuel, and Mark?"

Jemima frowned. "What I do is my own business, Deborah King," she said, with uncharacteristic tartness, "--not yours!"

"Fine," Deborah replied blandly, "but you can calm down. I'm not bashing your choice. I have to admit, he is a very nice-looking guy. Maybe not as good-looking as Joseph, or as well-built as Mark, but close. He's got plenty of nerve, I'll say that, he's smart, and he's *way* cooler than the other three.

"Are you planning *not* to join the church, and go Englisch, then?"

"Oh, for heaven's sake!" Jemima exclaimed crossly, "I'm not planning anything, and Brad Williams is not my choice, and I don't understand why you even brought him up."

Deborah smirked, "Please. I may be 14, but I'm not blind. I saw your face when you came back. After all your other romances, I know the *kissy face* look, and since Mark and Samuel and Joseph were all at work today -- it had to be the Englischer boy."

Jemima's mouth dropped open, and Deborah nodded, "*Mmmm-hmm.*"

Jemima swallowed, and tried not to look worried. "Why are you saying all this?"

Deborah shrugged. "I just wanted to tell you that I know and that I *approve*. In fact, I'll help you, if you like. I can talk him up to Mamm and Daed. You'll need that if you decide to keep seeing him."

Jemima frowned. "Why are you doing this? You're not – well, you don't *usually* –"

"I'm not usually *nice* to you," Deborah agreed. "True. But, maybe I've changed my ways."

Jemima frowned and gave her a narrow look: but Deborah only smiled angelically and walked out.

Jemima watched her go, then fell back onto the bed and gnawed her fingers. Now she was in Deborah's power -- as if she didn't already have enough troubles!

But even that danger couldn't distract her for long. After a few fretful minutes she drifted back into her dream: of being locked in Brad's embrace, of being kissed by that handsome madman, of feeling like they were all alone, like nothing and no one else *even existed.*

He had closed her in his arms and crushed her to his lips, in spite of the pain she knew it had cost him, and kissed her like a wild man. He had murmured in her ear, crazy things, had made her lose her breath, cry out even though they weren't alone, and made her promise that she'd meet him again after the trial. He had even promised to come back to their *house*, and she knew he was capable of doing it, in spite of the danger.

He might be an Englischer, but Brad Williams was a brave man, and a good and kind man. He had been amazingly unselfish, in spite of his talk about wanting a story for himself.

There was no *future* in Brad Williams, she knew that, but as long as he was there, as long as he kept coming back and holding out his hand, she would keep taking it. She frowned because it wasn't fair to Joseph, or Samuel, or Mark – but she couldn't help what she felt.

She trembled inside, thinking that maybe Brad had been right. Maybe if you loved someone – you knew *right away.*

She looked up at the ceiling and tried to pray, but God felt far away and remote. She had the guilty sense that she was doing wrong, or at least, doing *stupidly*. It wasn't wise for her to see an Englisch boy, because once she joined the church, she would only be able to marry another church member – not an outsider. And Brad Williams was *definitely* an outsider.

Her mother was right. She was setting herself up to be hurt. *None* of this was going to end well.

But as long as she could put off the painful ending, *she didn't care*. Jemima leaned over and blew out the light.

CHAPTER EIGHTEEN

Brad Williams unlocked the door to Room 321, took a running start, and jumped onto the bed with his arms flung out. Then he rolled over, stretched out, folded his arms behind his head, and laughed.

His cell phone buzzed, and he reached for it.

"*Hello, Brad,*" Delores' dry voice greeted him. "*You're* the one who's supposed to be calling *me* – remember? So how's it going? Have you talked to the girl yet?"

"I talked to her today, for a long time," he answered. "It wasn't an interview, but I'm back in. I'm pretty sure she'll tell me later if I ask."

Delores' voice sounded irritated. "Why didn't you just get the interview, while you *had* her? After all the trouble you've had making contact –"

"Trust me, Delores, I have to finesse this thing. The last time I saw her, she all but cussed me out. I'm coming in cold, after a long absence, and after a lot of bad things have happened. If I hit her again with a big request too soon, she'll bail, and we're out of luck."

There was a long, pregnant silence on the other end of the line. Brad could almost hear Delores' brain turning his words over, sniffing them.

"This wouldn't have anything to do with the fact that she's – what was the word you used – *photogenic* -- would it, Brad?" Delores drawled. "Because if I get the idea that you're stringing this assignment out to romance that girl, I'll –"

"I *promise* you, Delores," Brad replied smoothly, "I'm on the job. Just let me do things my own way."

Delores grumbled on the other end of the line. "You're taking a lot of chances, hot shot. You'd better be right."

"I've been right so far, haven't I?"

"You've been lucky. Meanwhile, Wellman at Channel 1 is running quotes from everyone in town who's ever *seen* her, and we have nothing."

Brad's smile faded. "Wellman has stories because he

makes up half of them," he retorted. "I'm handicapped, Delores. I have to wait until people actually *say* things."

To his surprise, she chuckled. "You're wasted on us, hot shot. You should work in PR. But remember – my patience is running thin. The public is interested in this story, but that will *only* last until the end of her court case. You have until then. Don't disappoint me."

There was a *click*.

Brad tossed the phone onto the bed, rolled his eyes up to the ceiling, put his hands on his head, and exhaled. He told himself that he *liked* to talk to Delores, because the end of the conversation always gave him a *near-death rush*.

He reached for the TV remote and the television winked to life. The local station was on commercial break. A car salesman named "Honest John" had dressed up as an Amish farmer and was poking "high prices" with a pitchfork.

Then the commercial ended, and the local news came on. It was the five o' clock broadcast.

To Brad's irritation, Wellman from Channel 1 was standing there with a mic to his face. Wellman was a tall, handsome specimen dressed in the reporter's uniform: a sports coat, a tie, slacks -- and a big gold ring. Brad noted that he had a more than *usually* bad case of reporter hair.

"And how do you know Jemima King?" he was asking. A teenaged girl was standing there, squinting into the camera.

"I saw her when she came to the hospital," the girl replied, smiling nervously. "I work in the gift shop, and she walked right past me. I recognized her because of her clothes. And her red hair."

"That was the day that she came to visit her friends, the Yoders," Wellman clarified, smiling directly into the camera. "Would you have guessed that she was there to give away *$200,000?*"

The girl shook her head. "I just thought she was there to see a doctor or something," she confessed.

Brad laughed out loud, and Wellman looked temporarily nonplussed. "Have you ever seen *anything like this before?*" he pressed, and the girl shook her head obligingly.

Finally, to wrap up the segment, he had the girl hold up a cloth doll. It was a red-haired Amish girl with angel wings. "What's this?" he asked, smiling into the camera.

"It's our 'Jemima' doll," the girl explained. "We can't keep them on the shelves."

"Well, she certainly does sound like an angel," Wellman replied. "And Channel 1 will be here to cover the $1.6 million dollar lawsuit being brought against her next week. Back to you, Monica."

Brad cursed under his breath and flicked a button on the remote. The TV went dead.

Brad closed his eyes and expelled all the breath in his body in one long, tired sigh. It was dinnertime, and he'd didn't feel like going down to the restaurant, so he grabbed the menu off the nightstand and picked up his phone again.

"Is this room service? Good. This is Room 321. Yeah, I'd like the steak burger meal. Sure, thirty minutes will be fine."

It was still early, but he was *in* for the evening. He was tired, mentally and physically, and he needed to recharge his brain if he hoped to get the scoop that Delores lusted after -- and that would save his job.

He pulled his hands over his face. He probably owed his job to the fact that he'd been able to charm Delores into giving him chances that no one else got. He had already missed one deadline.

Why *hadn't* he just gotten an interview from Jemima, when he had the chance? It was a fair question, and he didn't have an answer that made any sense to *him*, much less one that would satisfy Delores.

He opened his fingers and stared out through them. The truth, of course, was that being close to the Duchess had scrambled his brain, and he'd forgotten what he was supposed to be doing. He had forgotten why he was even *there*, and everything, in fact, except the urgent need to grab her and pick up where they'd left off.

It was a funny thing, too, because he wasn't the caveman type, usually. He liked to use his wits with women.

Except that when he was with the Duchess, he couldn't *find* them.

He shook his head. It was stupid, this whole thing: he was a moron, and he needed to get his head on straight, or he'd find himself in the unemployment line – as Delores had strongly hinted.

He put the phone back on the nightstand. The plain brown book was still lying there, where he left it. He picked it up idly and put it on his lap.

Jemima's soft voice echoed in his mind as he remembered their conversation:

I want what every Amish girl wants. To get married, to build a family. To live quietly, to be useful, to worship God in peace.

That last part is important to you, isn't it?

Of course.

He opened the plain brown book again. This time, it fell open more or less in the middle. He raised it just high enough to read: "Who can find a virtuous woman? For her price is far above rubies. The heart of her husband doth safely trust in her...She will do him good and not evil all the days of her life."

Brad let the book fall down again. He remembered his Mom, strung out on meth, slumped against the living room wall with her eyes rolled up to the ceiling and her mouth hanging open. His mouth twisted to one side.

But he couldn't get Jemima's soft voice out of his head. He heard it again, even when he closed his eyes and pulled a hand over his face:

I want what every Amish girl wants. To get married, to build a family. To live quietly, to be useful, to worship God in peace.

That last part is important to you, isn't it?

Of course.

CHAPTER NINETEEN

The next morning Brad went down to the hotel restaurant and enjoyed a leisurely breakfast and the morning paper. After a few days in Lancaster County, getting up *after* sunrise felt positively decadent.

He purused the front page of the *Lancaster Farmer's Friend*. It was a tiny local paper that had fallen into a big story by accident, but seemed to be playing it for all it was worth. The Duchess' upcoming court case was headline news, and the local slant was heavily in her favor. Brad noticed, with some satisfaction, that no one, even locally, had snagged a recent photo relevant to the story, except an extremely long-range shot of the King farmhouse.

Brad put down the paper and pulled out his smart phone. A quick scan online verified his hunch that it was the general trend. No one, not even Channel 1, had a picture of the Duchess, unless they had paid to display the one the *Ledger* had taken.

Brad took a sip of coffee and smiled to himself. He was on the brink of scooping even the networks because *no one* had the access to the Duchess that he enjoyed.

He sputtered suddenly and had to put the coffee cup down because a deep pain in his chest gave him an unholy jolt. It was that same pain he'd suffered before – the one deep down. It coincided with an intense feeling of guilt, but he pushed it away. *Guilt* was a luxury he couldn't afford, not if he wanted to keep his job.

He brushed coffee off of his shirt. But he had to admit that he did feel bad about – about what had happened earlier. If he'd had any sense, he wouldn't have tried to kiss the Duchess, or make her promises, but it was what always happened. He was an idiot.

Anyway, surely even an *Amish* girl had to understand that it was impossible for them to have anything more than a brief dalliance. She *had* to know that he was in this for the story. He'd told her often enough.

But he was looking forward to seeing her again. Or, to be honest, to seeing her for *one last time*. True, he'd screwed up, he shouldn't have made things *personal* between them, but maybe he could fix it. Maybe he could tell her that he'd been joking, or something, and encourage her to go back to her farm boys, so she wouldn't get the wrong idea.

But on the other hand, maybe she wouldn't *care* if he left. She'd told him that three other guys had proposed to her, so he probably wasn't even on her radar, at least not seriously.

He rubbed his jaw gingerly. Though, to be honest, he didn't *like* the idea of the Duchess ending up with that dark-haired guy. In fact, the mental image of the Duchess with anybody else was *No,* although he had the clarity to admit to himself that jealousy was insane. They hardly knew one another, and they weren't going to see each other at all after the court case.

In fact, Delores had been right – the sooner he got this interview *over with,* and himself out of Lancaster County, the better for everyone.

He paid his tab and returned to his room. He had just freshened up and was preparing to go out again when there was a soft knock on the hotel room door.

He frowned. He couldn't think of anyone who *should* be knocking.

He went to the door and opened it. To his amazement -- *Sheila* was standing there, in all her blonde glory.

"*Surprise,* Brad!" she purred, smiling from ear to ear. "*Guess who* just got assigned to help you on this story?"

Brad gaped at her. When his brain began to work again, it ran a frantic inventory of all the ways that having Sheila in his hair would destroy his chances of seeing the Duchess again. And one look at her face told him that Sheila *knew it*.

Brad pulled his mouth into a smile. "Sheila! What are *you* doing here? And what do you mean, *help me with this story*? You're *Delores'* assistant – aren't you?"

Sheila breezed past him and perched on the edge of a chair inside his room. "I'm *your* assistant now, Brad! Delores was so *sweet*, Brad, you wouldn't believe it. She said that she could see that I was *pining* for you, so she gave me permission to come here and help you with the story. She said that *you* need me more than *she* does – Wasn't that thoughtful of her?"

Brad laughed and nodded. "That Delores! Yeah, *that* – that Delores!" he agreed, looking up at the ceiling.

"And you know what's even better, Brad? The boy at the front desk was able to get me just a few doors down from you. So we can see each other all the time, for as long as we're here!"

He stared at her, and shook his head, and put his hands on his hips, and looked down at the carpet.

"That's – that's really great, Sheila!" he stammered.

She lifted her big blue eyes to his face. "So, Brad. How can I help you? I can see you've gotten into trouble already."

She lifted her hand to his chin and turned it carefully. "Poor thing! How did you get this shiner? Did one of the *Amish* people hit you?"

"Actually, *yes*, that happened. It's a long, strange story, Sheila, and I'd love to tell you all about it, but –"

Sheila nodded shrewdly. "But you have an urgent meeting and have to go, and why don't I just relax and wait for you back in my room?"

Brad mustered a sickly smile. "I knew you'd understand, Sheils," he told her warmly, "you're such a sport!" He made for the door, but she grabbed his tie as he passed.

"Nah, I want to come with you," she told him pleasantly. "So much more fun, don't you think? You can show me the back 40. Isn't that what they call it out here?" she giggled, and nibbled his ear.

He switched to another tack, "Ah – you know, this was a bit of a surprise, Sheils, but it works out *perfectly*! Because I was going to spend the morning at the library, doing research, but it would be time better spent getting interviews. Could *you* maybe spend the morning at the library? I'd want articles about former lawsuits in Lancaster County. I would *really* save me time."

She ran her hands through his hair.

"Not so fast, handsome. Because the last thing that Delores told me – bless her! – was that I'm supposed to stick to you *just like glue* until you get the Amish Dolly interview and *write your story*." She tapped his nose with a manicured finger. "And that's just what I intend to *do*."

Then she put her arms around him and kissed him with lips tasting of spearmint and strawberry gloss. Brad allowed himself to experience Sheila's kiss. He told himself that he and Sheila had a lot in common, that he was fond of her, they got along, he found her attractive.

And -- he still wished she was a *thousand miles away*.

And as for *Delores* -- Brad lifted his eyes to the ceiling. He had to give it to Delores, she was scary smart. She was crafty.

And he was going to get even with her for this, if it was his *dying act*.

CHAPTER TWENTY

The court case was scheduled for the following Monday, and there were a few days left before Brad would be called up to testify. He had hoped to talk to Jemima again, but instead, he found himself using the time to entertain Sheila.

She rapped on his door at 9 a.m. the following morning. Brad wiped shaving cream off of his chin, pulled on his belt, and stepped into his shoes. She was kind of early, but then, *early* was a relative term. If there was one thing he appreciated about Sheila, it was that she did *not* require him to battle the world before sunrise.

He opened the door, and Sheila was standing in the opening with one hand on the frame, and the other set jauntily on one hip. She smiled at him, and jingled her car keys.

He allowed himself to admire her. Sheila was a beautiful girl. On that particular morning, her hair was pulled back into a sleek ponytail, and she was wearing a little red number that hugged every curve. And Sheila *did* have the curves.

She was wearing a little more mascara and lipstick than he liked, but there was no denying that he was a lucky guy. Kind of.

Because Sheila required *attention.*

"Let's grab some breakfast," she was saying. "I saw a cute little B&B on the way in, and you can bring me up to speed on the way over."

He assumed an innocent expression. "Oh, there's *really* not that much to tell, Sheila," he said apologetically. "Actually, it's been kind of *dull*, out here in the green hill county. Not much to do," he laughed.

She gave him a shrewd look. "Yes, I can see that," she drawled, flicking his bruised chin with her finger. "You never *did* tell me how you got that mark."

Brad gave her a big, cheesy smile and cast about in his mind for the least damaging way to explain. "I met a stranger *by accident*," he joked.

"Good grief, Brad," she teased, "do you mean that one of the *locals* popped you? They're incredibly boring, but they aren't supposed to be *violent!*" she laughed.

He rubbed his jaw gingerly. "You'd be surprised," he muttered.

"*Hmmm*. Well, if I had to guess, I'd say it had something to do with the Amish Dolly," she sighed and smiled. "And we can't have that, now – *can* we?"

Then she leaned over, gave him a kiss, and pulled him outside by his tie.

They spent the better part of the morning at the Happy Daisy Rest B&B outside of town. The Happy Daisy Rest was a two-story white clapboard farmhouse that had been tricked out in frilly gingerbread trim, lavishly landscaped, and turned into a bed and breakfast by a retired couple.

Sheila ordered the full breakfast. It was overpriced, served on bone china, skimpy by the generous local standards, and slow to arrive because the owners insisted on serving it in five stages. It was a touch that seemed to delight Sheila, but that Brad found pretentious and irritating.

Sheila devoured a cheese and spinach quiche about the size of a half-dollar, dabbed her lips, and cast an approving glance around the dining room. "You know, Brad, I can almost see it, why people come here. It's like taking a vacation to 1875. It might actually be *relaxing* for a day or two when things get crazy in the city."

Brad nodded silently and popped a biscuit that was small enough to be eaten in one bite.

"But I would think that after that, you'd just *lose your mind* with boredom," she added, taking a sip of coffee.

Brad smiled, nodded, and raised his own cup.

He was mostly silent, but since Sheila more than filled the gap with office gossip, he wasn't required to come up with much conversation. That was a relief: because there wasn't much he could *afford* to tell her.

Sheila continued to talk. After a leisurely half hour they finished their meal, and the owner brought the check. Brad reached into his wallet for his card.

Sheila picked up the tab, glanced at it, and giggled. *"We're in luck!"* she whispered. *"Look – they forgot to charge us for the second meal. Score!"*

Brad raised his eyebrows. He would've thought nothing of letting it slide a month ago, back in the city. But here, in the middle of Amish country, the small dishonesty seemed glaringly wrong.

Brad smiled awkwardly, because his reason sounded lame, even to him. "I can't stiff them, Shiels," he told her and raised his hand. "*Sir?*"

Sheila leaned in and hissed: "What are you doing? It was overpriced – you're blocking karma!"

But by that time, the owner had come to the table. Brad looked up at him sheepishly. He felt like a fool but made himself say: "Um – our bill was only for one meal, instead of two."

The man peered at it and gasped. "You're right – and *thank you*! I appreciate your honesty!"

The man hurried off to correct the mistake, and Sheila gave him a disgusted look. "What's wrong with you? You could have saved the paper some money!"

He shrugged sheepishly. "Must be something in the water around here," he told her, and got up to go.

Brad soon discovered that Sheila had a full itinerary for the day, and after breakfast she drove into downtown Serenity for some shopping. She hinted strongly that he should come, *too*.

Brad smiled and told her *no* as politely as he could muster. "People know my face around here," he shrugged. "I don't want them to mob me about Jemima."

Sheila raised her brows. "*Oh* yes – the Amish Dolly. She's the hometown hero here, isn't she?" she drawled. "That must be so irritating for you, Brad! I guess you're counting the days until you can get *out* of here, and back to *civilization*. Well, it won't be too long now – poor darling!"

She leaned over to give him a peck on the cheek. "Don't

go too far now! I'll meet you back at the gazebo in the square, in an hour."

Brad nodded, and waved, and Sheila teetered off on her three-inch heels. She had soon disappeared into one of Serenity's many gift shops.

And as soon as she was gone, Brad turned into an alley between buildings and dug in his pocket for his cell phone. He opened his messages and searched down them with a hungry eye. He'd given the Duchess his cell phone number and asked her to call him if she thought she could get away. To his disappointment, there was no message.

He sighed. Jemima's court case was going to be a media zoo, and he wanted to get the interview with her before then if he could. First and foremost, because Delores had threatened his job if he didn't; and secondly, because he had the feeling he might not get the chance to see Jemima afterward.

And he *really* wanted to see her one last time.

Of course, it was a lunatic desire: The Duchess was probably off with one of her farm boys at that very moment. She might even have decided which of them she wanted to *marry* by now. And it made perfect sense. They could give her what she wanted – a safe, quiet life and a family.

For an instant he allowed himself to picture what that would be like: living in the gorgeous green hill country, leading the simple life, turning his back on the 21st century with all of its noise and tension. No crushing deadlines, no games, no cutthroat competition. One day of peace melting into another, with familiar faces all around.

And for just an instant -- because he couldn't keep himself from doing it -- he imagined waking up to the Duchess' angel face every morning, of having her soft voice be the first sound to touch his ear. He closed his eyes and smiled.

After a long, pleasant moment, Brad opened his eyes again, turned the phone off and put it back into his pocket, frowning. He twisted his mouth sardonically. He'd never known anything even *close* to that pleasant dream. And if the truth were told, the Amish hinterland probably wasn't as perfect as it looked from the outside. Most things weren't.

And then, too, the Amish had all that religious guilt. They had to worship all the time, and their faith required endless hand-wringing about "sin." Even though, comparatively speaking, they probably needed to repent the *least* of anyone within a thousand miles. Or, the *particular* Amish person that he was thinking of, anyway.

He sighed and looked up at a small sliver of sky between the alley walls. No, Sheila was right, Delores was right, and *he* was right – in his moments of clarity. The Duchess was nothing but a beautiful mirage.

And a heck of a good *story*. The sooner he started thinking of her that way, the better.

But when he turned to leave the alley between the two stores, he happened to pass one of the display windows. There, with its big green eyes looking out at him, was the innocent Jemima doll, with its wispy red hair and angel wings.

CHAPTER TWENTY-ONE

It was still dark when the cell phone alarm went off in Brad's ear. It felt like no time had passed at all from the previous night. Brad groaned and pulled his hands down over his face. For about five minutes he told himself that it wasn't all that big a deal to get away from Sheila, But six minutes was all it took for him to think better of that, and to plant his feet on the floor.

He hated getting up early, and he'd have to find some way to play it off with Sheila later, but *one day* was all that he was willing to spend on shopping and overpriced food. And he was reasonably certain that Sheila didn't rise before the sun.

He stumbled to the bathroom and took a quick shower,

shaved, and dressed. He felt half-alive, but by local standards it wasn't even all that early. In the Englisch world, it might still be the night before, but at 5 a.m., Lancaster County was open for business.

When he was shaved and brushed and dressed and combed, Brad quietly locked his hotel room and padded down to Sheila's door. He pushed a small note under it, then descended the metal stairs to the breezeway, and walked out to the truck. He slid in, cranked the engine, and escaped to the freedom of the open road.

He rolled down the windows on the truck and let the cool air of early fall come pouring in. The hotel was well outside of town and mostly surrounded by rolling fields. They were beautiful at that time of year, thick with corn, and even at that early hour, there were boys out in them, driving teams ahead of a harvester.

He turned his head to watch them as the fenceposts flashed past: they were sitting up on the rigs, holding the reins. From where he was, it almost looked as if they were sailing across endless green waves.

He shook his head, smiling. It was picturesque, he had to admit it. He was going to miss that part when he went home to his studio apartment in the city.

He pulled the truck into the parking lot of a little cafe on the outskirts of town. It was already crowded, even though the sun was just rising, and he was lucky to find a window booth. The prospect faced out onto one of those endless fields, brushed by the new gold of the dawning sun. A pretty waitress came over and smiled at him. "Good morning! What can I get for you?"

"*Coffee*," he replied instantly, "*black* coffee. Ham and gravy biscuits, scrambled eggs with cheese, hash browns, and – let's see – a side of bacon."

"Coming up." He reached into his pocket and pulled out his smart phone. To his surprise, there was an instant message from Sheila. It read: *Ha ha, Brad, very funny.*

He grinned but declined to answer: because when he did, he was going to have to strike just the right balance of groveling apology, and firmness, and truly *creative* replies took time.

To his surprise, and delight, the waitress brought his order back in less than five minutes – platter after platter of good, solid farm food, trailing fragrant steam. He set to immediately, and almost closed his eyes in deep appreciation. This part of the country understood food.

He gave the plate his undivided attention for better than 15 minutes. That was another thing he was going to miss when he left: good, simple food, and plenty of it.

His phone buzzed, and he picked it up, thinking that Sheila must have thought of something else, but the message was from the lawyer, Hutchinson. The old shark wanted him to come in for a *briefing* before Jemima's court cast – legalese for "coaching." He took another bite of ham.

He was about the shut the phone completely off, but there was another notification on his call list. It was sandwiched in between the other two, and he almost missed it. But there, in black and white, was the number he'd almost forgotten.

The call had been from *Jemima*.

He coughed, and spilled coffee on himself, and cursed, and brushed it off with his napkin. He fumbled with the phone and pressed it to his ear.

Her voice was so soft that he could hardly make it out over the background noise in the diner, and he cupped his hand over the phone. He could just make out:

"...might not see you after, so I thought we might talk one more time. You can come to the same place as last time, in the garden. My parents are going to town so no one will see. I will be there today."

There was a long pause, and then, even fainter than before, two unintelligible words, then a click. He cursed and played the message back again, and they were still unintelligible. He played it a third time, and this time he was able to hear them.

"*Please come.*"

He sat there, with his mouth open, not quite believing his own ears. Then he played the message back a fourth time.

There it was -- faint but real.

"Please come."

He stared at the tabletop without really seeing it. His pulse was beating in his neck, his mouth was dry, and the brain was blank.

"Please come."

He came to with a start, checked his watch. It was just coming up on 7 o'clock – midmorning, in these parts.

He slapped a $20 down on the table, took a quick sip of coffee, and left.

It was a fairly short drive from town to the King farm. Brad took his usual route, parking next to the overgrown tract of land next door, and hiked over the bramble bushes to the fenceline. He gave the yard and the house a quick sweep. There was no one visible, and no sounds of hammering, so he jumped over.

He made his way through the undergrowth, and so almost walked right into Jemima. She was standing there in the deep undergrowth beyond the garden – well hidden from anyone who might be watching from the house.

The suddenness of her appearance took his breath. He

pulled up short, mustered a lopsided smile, and tried not to look as goofy as he felt.

"*Duchess!*" he exclaimed -- absurdly. She was standing there, bathed in golden morning light, like some flame-haired pre-Raphaelite vision, and framed by a curtain of golden fall leaves. He wanted to stare at her but forced himself to concentrate.

"I –*um* -- I got your message," he stammered. "I'm glad you called. I wanted to talk to you, *too*."

He lifted his head and looked around. "Where can we talk?"

She smiled at him softly. "We can go to the house. My parents are gone. *Come*."

To his amazement, she reached out and took his hand. Hers was soft and warm as a kitten's, and almost as small.

He followed her across the lawn, past the garden, and up the porch. She led him to the porch swing and sat down on it. He sat down quickly beside her.

She released his hand, and put her own in her lap, and looked down at them without speaking for a long while.

In that long silence, his brain slowly woke up. He had to keep his head on straight. He had to remember Delores' warnings; his *job* was riding on whether or not he could get this interview. He hated to do it, but he *had* to do it.

He reached down into his pocket, and gently pushed a spot on the phone screen. The recording app kicked in.

Jemima looked up at him with those soft green eyes, the one that tilted up at the edges, the ones that seemed bottomless.

"I wanted to thank you," she said at last. "For everything. And to say I'm sorry for the bad things that happened to you. It's hard to us to trust outsiders. So many of them have not been kind."

Guilt twisted in his chest. He smiled a sickly smile. "It's alright," he assured her.

She added: "We won't be seeing much of each other after next week, maybe." She paused, as if waiting for him to refute it, but he forced himself not to answer. It wouldn't be fair to her.

She bowed her head and went on: "So I will tell you what happened. Mr. Morton came out ahead of you that day, and he only told me that he wanted the clock. He was very impatient. But I never promised to sell it to him."

He nodded. "I know."

"After you left, I thought about what you had said. About the letter being valuable, maybe. But I didn't see why that was so important. I didn't see why everyone was so excited. So I sent it to you. And I thought that you would take it."

She paused again, not looking up.

"But you didn't take it. And I was very surprised. So I – went along, with what you said. Mostly because I – I wanted to know *why* you hadn't taken the letter."

Brad looked up at the ceiling and tightened his lips to a thin line.

"I *still* don't know why you didn't take it."

Brad looked down at her, mustered a smile. "Call it *hochmut*, Duchess," he said gently.

She nodded and went on. "And when we went to the city, when we were watching the auction, and the price kept going up and up, I could see that you were thinking about the letter. And about giving it up. It must have been very hard, to give it up."

Brad pulled back, crossed his legs, coughed. He knew that he needed to start asking her questions, to begin guiding the conversation in the direction he needed it to go, but somehow he couldn't bring himself to do it.

"And after the auction was over. I think I know what you did, when we were there," she murmured, "*now*. You were taking me away before the *other* reporters could come, and – and take pictures, and shoot videos, and ask more questions."

She lifted her eyes to his face. "Isn't that right?"

He tried to make his mouth move into a smile, but it

wouldn't obey. He looked down and didn't answer.

"When the story came out, and all the people came here, it was very hard. I didn't understand why they thought it was so important, to have more money than everybody else. As if I had done something *wonderful*, when I had only bought a clock."

She picked at the fabric of her apron. "The elders had to go to the police, to ask them to block the roads, so many people came here. All because of the money. People I had never met, writing letters, and calling on the phone, and coming out to the house. Daed had to protect us, or they would have come inside our house."

"I can't tell you how sorry I am for that, Jemima," he said quietly.

She tilted her head to one side and shrugged. "It wasn't your fault. You only wrote a story. The rest was other people."

She sighed, and straightened. "Then one day a man came out and asked for me. He threw some papers at me and ran away. The papers were about the lawsuit. And that was hard, too. Because I don't have all the money anymore. I gave a lot of it away already. And I thought about it and prayed about it.

"We're not supposed to sue, you know," she told him. "And my Mamm was very upset, when I told her I was going to get a lawyer. But I believe that God told me to *give the money to other people.* And I can't do that if I don't have it anymore."

She looked up at him with those doe eyes. "What do you think?" she asked.

Brad didn't trust himself to reply. He coughed again, and looked away. "I think you're right," he said at last.

She nodded. "So I'm going to court. And that will be hard, too. But, I'm very grateful that you – came forward to tell the judge about what you heard. It was very nice."

Brad looked off into the distance and shrugged awkwardly.

"I'm sorry that I said mean things about you, and that I thought them. Because you really have been very – *kind*," she said firmly.

She looked up at him again. "I would offer you the money again, if I thought you would take it," she sighed. "But because I know you will *not*, I'll give you something else you want.

"I'll give you what I just said. I know that you're taping me somehow, Brad Williams. But I make you a gift of it."

Then she leaned forward, put a hand to his chin, and kissed him. Then she rose and went inside the house, leaving him to stare after her.

CHAPTER TWENTY-TWO

Brad spent that evening holed up in his hotel room. He locked the door behind him, sat cross-legged on his bed, and opened his laptop. Then he reached into his pocket, pulled out the phone, and pushed a button. Jemima's soft voice trickled out into the silence of the room.

"I wanted to thank you for everything. And to say I'm sorry for the bad things that happened to you."

Brad stuck a cigarette into his mouth and started to type and chain smoke. He typed and retyped all through the night until the laptop was hot enough to make it a fire hazard, and the ashtray on the bedside table was overflowing.

By the time the sun was rising, Brad had finished. He hit the "send" button, sighed deeply, and stretched out across the bed, where he instantly fell deeply asleep.

He woke up hours later, roused by the shrieks of children playing and splashing in the pool below his bedroom window. It was broad daylight – *noon*, in fact.

He opened the laptop again. His inbox was overflowing with messages, mostly from Delores, which he ignored. But there was one message from Sheila, and after long hesitation, he opened it.

Dear Brad,

I read your article. I'll say this for you, you're creative. This has to be one of the most unusual Dear Jane letters I've ever read. But I do understand that's what it is, as least as far as it concerns me. It made me shed a tear, even, and that doesn't happen often. But don't worry – I'm not a girl who mopes around.

Well, handsome, it was fun, and it was worth a try. If you ever change your mind, I'll be around. You can give me a call anytime.

XOXO,

Sheila

Brad stood up and took a few paces to the window. Sure

enough, her car was gone. He sat down on the bed, sighed again, and pulled his hands over his face. Sheila's beautiful blue eyes shimmered in his imagination for an instant, then faded.

Then he opened his eyes, scrolled down to his employer's messages, and read them, one after another. Delores' emails were much more to the point.

Brad,

If you don't get that article to me within the next 24 hours, you'll be reporting to the unemployment office.

Brad,

What's this I hear about you testifying in that girl's trial? If I find out that you're trying to make yourself a name by becoming a part of this story, I will fire you.

Brad lit another cigarette, blew a puff of smoke to the ceiling and frowned. How had Delores found *that* out?

Brad,

You've got exactly three more hours. Don't make me come down there myself.

Brad,

Finally! I'll message you when I'm finished reading it. After all the time you spent on this, it had better be good.

Brad,

This is in the wrong format. It's supposed to be a feature article, not an editorial. But it's brilliant, so I'll let you get away with it, just this once. We'll see how it plays, but my guess is that it'll go wildfire, like the other one. Congratulations, wonder boy.

P.S. Clever of you. An editorial doesn't require another photo – don't think I didn't notice the trick!

P.P.S.

I expect you in the office on Monday morning, bright and early.

Brad sputtered, and a wavy line of smoke curled out into the air. He was going to be in court on Monday so Delores would have to be patient. He turned back to the laptop and scrolled down further. There was also a message from the lawyer.

Dear Mr. Williams:

This is to remind you that you have a consultation with Mr. Hutchinson on Friday at 12:30 regarding the Jemima King trial on Monday morning. Mr. Hutchinson looks forward to talking to you then.

Regards,

Law Office of Barfield Hutchinson

Brad closed out of the email window, checked his watch, cursed, and jumped up from the bed. He only had a few minutes to shower, shave and dress.

In less than ten minutes he had shrugged into his coat, jumped into his shoes, and slammed the hotel room door behind him. But the laptop on the bedside table was still open to a file titled "Jemima King."

My Epiphany

by Brad Williams

"As a reporter, it's necessary to be objective – to distance yourself from the events that you describe. To some extent, it's like being a doctor or a nurse: you have to step back, or the ugliness that you witness will make you numb, and eventually, useless.

But how do you remain objective to beauty – to exquisite, transcendent beauty? This reporter has been trying to do that for months now, and can testify that it's impossible.

When I was first assigned to cover the remarkable story of Jemima King – the Amish girl who became a millionaire when she discovered a rare letter – I thought it would be just another story. I didn't think that it would change my life. But it did.

Ledger readers will remember that this Amish girl sold the letter at Brinkley's for $1.6 million dollars. What they don't know is that this historic sale almost never happened.

Because this Amish girl really doesn't believe that having a great deal of money is all that important.

Don't believe it? I didn't either, at first. But I quickly learned that Miss King meant what she said. In fact, at the beginning of our acquaintance -- and after she understood how much it was worth -- Miss King tried to give the letter away.

To *me*.

She offered again yesterday when I spoke to her about her upcoming trial. You see, Miss King is being sued for the whole $1.6 million by a man who claims that she promised to sell the letter to him and reneged. Not everyone is as indifferent to a million dollars as Miss King.

Jemima King has been in the news recently, and deservedly so – she has donated more than half a million dollars to neighbors and friends whose medical bills far exceeded their ability to pay. She has been rightly praised as a generous, selfless person. And yet, when I spoke to her, she seemed puzzled.

She told me: "I didn't understand why (people) thought it was so important, to have more money than everybody else. As if I had done something wonderful, when I had only bought a clock."

I tried to think of an answer to that, and couldn't. Because while there may be nothing praiseworthy about receiving a sudden windfall, it is extraordinarily selfless and remarkable to spend hundreds of thousands of dollars on others in need.

Anyone who has seen Miss King, or even her photograph, will observe that she is physically beautiful. Yet she is one of those rare people who is also beautiful on the inside.

Which brings me to the title of this editorial. Meeting Miss King was an epiphany for me, in the truest sense of the world. Before I met her, I was an agnostic. But I have changed my views.

Because I have confirmed the existence of an angel, I must therefore now concede the corresponding existence of a God.

How is it possible to remain objective to beauty, to remain unmoved by ineffable grace and generosity? I have discovered that it's impossible, and amid all the scandals and wars and tragedies of our world, this is the most hopeful news that I have ever been privileged to report."

CHAPTER TWENTY-THREE

Brad Williams shifted his weight from one leg to the other and looked up into the grave blue eyes of Barfield Hutchinson.

It was Monday morning, and the courthouse was jammed. Brad scanned the courtroom. Just beyond the big double doors, the press, a good deal of the Amish community, and hordes of curious paparazzi-filled the halls outside.

Inside, the benches were full as well – at least on Jemima's side of the room. Caldwell Morton and his attorney sat on one side, and Jemima, her family, and what looked like at least forty Amish friends and family filled the other side.

"How did you meet Miss King?" Hutchinson asked, clasping his hands behind his back.

Brad leaned toward the microphone in front of the witness box. "I was in downtown Serenity to cover a fair for my employer, the *Ledger* newspaper."

"You're a reporter there, are you not?"

"That's right."

"And what happened on the day that you first met her?"

"I went into the Satterwhite Gift Shop to grab a bite to eat before the fair opened, and Miss King was just walking out. We bumped into one another by accident, and the clock she was holding fell to the ground and a piece of paper fell out of it. I reached down and picked them up for her."

"But neither you, nor Miss King, saw what the paper was?"

"I didn't, and Miss King didn't even look at it. She took the clock and left immediately."

The lawyer nodded. Brad allowed his eyes to wander momentarily. Jemima was sitting on the defendant's bench. Her huge father – who seemed crammed into his black coat – and her mother, a very pretty blonde woman, were in the row immediately behind her.

Brad's glance flitted beyond them, to the people sitting on the back rows. He noticed the guy with the black hair and was gratified to see the remains of a truly epic shiner on his left eye. The guy with the silly straw hat was also there, and a third guy – a blonde – looked as if he might be the last of the Duchess' admirers.

Because *all* of them were staring at him like they wished they could jump the rails and swing at him.

"And what happened after Miss King left?"

Brad cleared his throat. "I went into the shop and bought something to eat. There was no place to sit, so I stood in the doorway. Then Mr. Morton came in, and nearly knocked me down."

"And why was that?"

"He was in a hurry," Brad replied, throwing Morton a dry glance. "He asked the shop owner if he'd bought an antique clock recently, and the man said he had. Morton was very anxious to get it. He asked the shop owner if he could get the name of the person who had bought it, but the man wouldn't give it to him."

Brad paused, and glanced over at the jury to see how his words were going over. The people in the jury box looked like local people, and to judge from their expressions, they were sympathetic to Jemima. Though Brad couldn't imagine how anyone could *avoid* that.

He glanced at her. She was sitting with her hands clasped in her lap. She hadn't looked up at all during the previous testimony, but her eyes had been trained on his face from the moment he sat down in the box.

Hutchinson pursed his lips and nodded. "So it was clear that Miss King had bought the clock earlier?"

"Yes."

"And that Mr. Morton wanted the clock urgently?"

Brad shot Morton a withering glance. "Oh yeah."

"What happened after that?"

"Morton left, and I thought it was funny that he wanted the clock so badly. I figured there might be a story in it, so I asked around for the directions to Miss King's house. I wanted to see if the clock was valuable, or something. I suspected that was why Morton wanted it."

"And so you went out to the King farm?" Hutchinson pressed.

"Yes."

"What happened then?"

"When I got there, Morton was ahead of me. I saw Miss King and Morton standing on the front porch of her house. He seemed agitated. He was talking loudly and pointing to the clock. When I got closer, I introduced myself and asked if I could talk to Miss King."

"How did Mr. Morton react?"

"He got mad. He told me that it was a private matter between him and Miss King and that he was about to buy the clock from her. I told her that she shouldn't sell it until she at least found out what the paper was. That made Morton even more upset. He said that Miss King had promised to sell the clock to him."

"And what did Miss King say?"

"She told him that she had *not* promised to sell the clock to him. Only to show it."

Hutchinson lifted his eyes to the jury box. "Can you repeat that, please, Mr. Williams?"

Brad leaned to the mic and stared into Caldwell Morton's face. "She said that she had only promised to *show it to him*."

"How did Mr. Morton react?"

"He flipped out. He threw money on the floor and said that the clock had belonged to his mother, that was rightfully his. When I told him that she had a right to keep it, he came at me."

Hutchinson raised his snowy eyebrows and affected surprise. "Mr. Morton became physically violent?"

"He pulled his fist back like he was going to slug me. I probably would've had to fight him, if her father hadn't shown up and thrown him out."

"I see. Thank you, Mr. Williams," Hutchinson smiled. "I

have no more questions."

He walked away and sat down beside Jemima. He leaned over and whispered something in Jemima's ear. She nodded.

Mr. Morton's attorney stood up. He was a small, thin man, with iron-gray hair, square glasses, and a mustache. He walked over and seemed to be reading from papers inside a manila folder.

"You said that you're a reporter for the *Ledger*, Mr. Williams?"

"Yes."

"Would you call yourself an objective reporter?"

Brad looked up at him. "I try to be."

"How well would you say you succeed?"

Brad gave the man a direct look. "I don't understand the question."

The lawyer lifted a newspaper over his head for the room to see. "I am holding a copy of the *Ledger* newspaper from last Friday. It contains an editorial entitled, 'My Epiphany.' Did you write this editorial, Mr. Williams?"

Brad looked at him. "Yes."

The lawyer walked over and placed the folded paper on top of the witness box. "Would you be so good as to read it, so we can all hear it?"

Brad could feel himself going red, and shot Hutchinson a questioning look, but the older man remained unmoved. Brad took the paper reluctantly, uncrossed his legs, and cleared his throat.

"As a reporter, it's necessary to be objective – to distance yourself from the events that you describe." He coughed, and slowly read the entire editorial in a voice that he hoped sounded neutral. It was odd, but it had been far easier to write those words for the whole world to read than to read them in front of Jemima and her family.

When he was finished, he looked up, folded the paper, and placed it back on top of the witness box. The lawyer walked over, took it in his hand, and held it up again.

"Mr. Williams has just said that it's important to be *objective*," the lawyer told the courtroom. "But it doesn't sound as if he's *at all* objective about Miss King! In this editorial" – he adjusted his glasses – "he calls her an 'angel,' a 'generous, selfless person,' 'remarkable,' and 'physically beautiful.'" The lawyer turned to face him.

"You did write those things, didn't you, Mr. Williams?"

Brad met his eyes steadily. "Yes, I did."

The lawyer turned to address the jury. "And yet, you expect us to believe that a young man so clearly smitten with Miss King can be a reliable witness in a case that concerns her?"

Hutchinson stood up. "*Objection -- argumentative!*"

The judge turned to face the lawyer. "Sustained."

The lawyer nodded slightly toward the judge and shrugged. "Mr. Williams, you admit that Miss King tried on two occasions to give you a great deal of money?"

Hutchinson bounced up again. "*Objection!*"

The judge glanced at him. "Overruled."

Brad set his jaw. "She told me at the beginning that she had no wish to be rich, and mailed me the original letter, as a gift, and without any conditions attached. And just last week, she offered to give me the rest of the money she had."

"That *is* remarkable," the lawyer agreed. "An Amish girl offers an outsider a *fortune*, when it's unusual for an Amish woman to even *speak* to a non-Amish man. Why do you suppose she did that, Mr. Williams?"

Brad turned to look at Jemima. Her face was raised to his, and her eyes on him were like stars, like green gems glittering under a jeweller's lamp.

"I have no reason to doubt her own explanation," Brad replied. "She has no desire to be rich, and her actions since then have proved it on multiple occasions."

"I see. But isn't there another, equally simple explanation, Mr. Williams? One that would certainly explain her desire to give you gifts, and your willingness to come here, and to testify on her behalf? Isn't it possible -- and in light of this information -- even *likely*, that Miss King is smitten with you?"

Hutchinson rose again, wearily. "*Objection!*"

"Sustained."

The lawyer glanced at the jury, smiled, and sat back down again. "I have no further questions, your honor."

CHAPTER TWENTY-FOUR

Brad stood up and walked to the back of the courtroom. He could feel Jemima's eyes on him as he passed, and he tried hard *not* to imagine what she was thinking.

His testimony had been the last, and he sat down on the back bench and settled in for the closing arguments. He figured that he was already in it up to his neck with Delores, so a few extra hours, more or less, would make little difference.

Morton's lawyer got up and argued that Mr. Morton's family had owned the letter for hundreds of years and that it had been lost by accident. He said that Jemima had acquired it through a mistake and that she promised to sell the letter to his client, and had reneged. The lawyer also claimed that his *own* eyewitness testimony was suspect because he was besotted with Jemima and therefore not a trustworthy witness.

Brad pulled his hands over his face, imagining how *that* was going to play back at the office, and how it would affect his reputation as a reporter. Not well, that was for sure, but he told himself he'd made the choice to do it, and he wasn't sorry.

After Morton's attorney was finished, Hutchinson stood up and, in Brad's opinion, destroyed the prosecution by arguing that Jemima had the receipt proving she bought the clock legally; that by the testimony of two witnesses, she had been in possession of the letter at the time of dispute; and that, according to his own testimony, she had not promised to sell the clock.

Hutchinson stood facing the jury and pointed dramatically to Jemima as she sat in the defendant's box. "Ladies and gentlemen of the jury, I ask you," he said grandly, "if innocence could reveal itself to the naked eye, could it wear a clearer face than the one you see before you?"

In spite of his feelings toward Jemima, Brad lowered his head and smirked into his shirt. Hutchinson should've had his own TV show, but in this case, Brad figured that even overripe rhetoric couldn't blow Jemima's chances. One look at her face, as Hutchinson had claimed, really *was* it all it took.

Hutchinson finally sat down, and the jury left the room to deliberate. Brad sighed and dug into his pocket for the smart phone. It might be hours before they came back. He checked his email messages. To his dismay, they were almost all from Delores.

Brad,

Where are you? I told you to be here this morning bright and early. If you're where I think you are, you can turn in your badge!

Brad stifled a groan and scrolled down.

Brad,

On second thought, if you're at the trial, make yourself useful. If you can get me a blow-by-blow by noon, I'll forgive you, but only if you get it to me fast.

Brad,

Are you reading your mail?

He sighed, turned off the phone, and stuck it into his pocket. Time passed.

Brad amused himself by studying his neighbors. The people around him were mostly local folk, and a good many were Amish. The row he was sitting on was empty except for him, but the others were filled with primly-dressed men and women. They were talking softly in that near-German dialect he'd heard Jemima use.

His gaze wandered, and he noticed that one of the black-clad figures was staring back at him. It was the tall blonde guy that he figured for one of Jemima's boyfriends, the one who'd been giving him the dead eye. The guy looked even more disapproving now -- if that was *possible*.

On an evil impulse, Brad made eye contact, cracked a wide grin and winked at him. The other young man scowled, drew himself up, and stood briefly, just before the door opened and the jury returned.

The young man was forced to sit back down again, but he gave Brad such a speaking look that Brad began to wonder if he'd been smart to push him. Still, it *had* been hard to resist. He chuckled to himself, shook his head, and rubbed his hands together.

He checked his watch; the jury had been gone almost no time at all – less than 20 minutes. It was either some technical glitch or they'd decided in record time. Brad took a look at their faces, and decided it was probably -- record time.

The judge addressed the foreman. "Have you reached a verdict?"

A portly middle-aged man stood up and nodded. "We have, your honor."

"How do you find?"

"We find in favor of the defendant."

Brad grinned and turned to leave. He brushed past the bailiffs, opened the doors a crack, and was promptly mobbed by the reporters who were waiting outside.

Amish Millionaire Cleared in $1.6 Million Suit

By Brad Williams

Serenity, PA – In a 12-0 decision, a jury today rejected Caldwell Morton's claim that Jemima King, the Amish millionaire, had promised to sell him a letter written by George Washington. The jury, made up of six men and six women, took only 20 minutes to clear Miss King of the charge.

The jury heard arguments from the prosecution lawyer, William Harwell, that the Morton family had owned the letter for hundreds of years, and that Miss King had obtained it when the clock had mistakenly been included in an estate sale.

Defense attorney Barfield Hutchinson countered by arguing that Miss King had produced a receipt for the clock, and that according to the testimony of several witnesses, was in lawful possession of the clock at the time of the dispute.

Several witnesses testified on behalf of Miss King, including Eli Satterwhite, the owner of Satterwhite's Gift Shop in Serenity, Penn.; who said that he sold Miss King the clock; John Maxwell, of Brinkley's Auction House in

Philadelphia, who testified that Miss King had produced valid evidence of ownership prior to the letter auction; and Brad Williams, of the *Ledger* newspaper, who testified that he had heard Miss King refuse to sell the letter to Morton when asked.

Miss King has given more than $500,000 to help local families pay medical bills, and has expressed her intention of giving the rest of her windfall to people in need.

Back in his hotel room, Brad hit the "send" button and checked his watch. It was 11:55. He'd saved his job with five minutes to spare.

He smiled, thinking that testifying on Jemima's behalf was the one thing he'd done since coming to Amish country that he felt completely good about. At least now, he'd done something that really *helped* her.

The rest – well, it was probably better to chalk it up to experience. His time with the Duchess had shown him little more than that he could be reduced to babbling idiocy by a pretty face, that he wanted what he thought he couldn't have, and that he didn't have the sense to keep a girl that he actually got along with, and who understood him.

Now, after all these reverses, it was time to return to the real world, and get back to his own life. He pulled his suitcase out from underneath the bed and opened it beside him.

His smartphone buzzed, and he glanced down at it. Delores had sent him an email.

Brad,

Great article. Here's something that will make you laugh: your editorial has gone viral on social media. You are now the lovelorn boy. Go and see what women are offering to send you in the mail, Romeo!

Brad raised his brows and sputtered out a laugh. He was about to put the phone down again, when the phone buzzed a second time. This time, it was a call.

He picked it up. "Hello?"

There was a long pause on the other end. "Brad?"

He sat up straight. Every nerve in his body was suddenly on alert. *It was Jemima.* How had she gotten hold of a phone?

"Yes, I'm here."

There was silence again. "I was hoping – I was hoping I could see you again, before you leave."

His heart was pounding. "Sure, that would be *great*. I can be at your house in say, twenty minutes."

"No…tonight. After ten o'clock. Could you come then?"

He went completely still and felt his heart beating.

"Sure."

There was a scuffling sound on the other end, a soft sound that might or might not have been a word, and then a dial tone.

CHAPTER TWENTY-FIVE

Brad spent the afternoon in his hotel room, cursing, arguing with himself, and chain smoking. He told himself that he was an idiot, that he should've told the Duchess that he had to leave, that it wasn't fair to Jemima or to himself to drag out a long goodbye. They had no chance, no future, and no good purpose was served by going over to her house at night.

Except that she had *asked* him to come, and apparently, he was her slave, like those three pitiful farm boys.

So he'd gone down to the desk and paid for an extra night on his own dime, like a moron, because the paper had only paid the room until noon. And settled in, and binge-watched the news, and ignored more emails from Delores, mostly to keep himself from speculating about *what Jemima wanted.*

Just to say goodbye, he was sure: but what form would that goodbye take? The possibilities were many and delightful, and sometimes he closed his eyes and let himself imagine them.

The afternoon wore on. Delores sent more emails, hinting that his recent successes did not make him immune to disciplinary action. She informed him that he'd ruined her secretary for any useful work, and suggested that he might want to see some of the packages being sent to his desk by anonymous admirers.

Brad ignored them, as well. He stretched out on the bed with the TV remote in his hand, flipping idly from channel to channel. He had scooped all the other news outlets with his exclusive interview with Jemima, and he was gratified to see that even Wellman at Channel 1 hadn't been able to do much better than awkward interviews with her random acquaintances.

He shook his head and smiled. He had to give them one thing: the Amish were a tight-knit people.

His smile faded. He tried to imagine what was he was going to say to Jemima that night. He could tell her that she was beautiful, that she was amazingly generous, that he genuinely admired the way she lived out what she believed.

That it was a shame that they weren't…

He crushed out his cigarette in the ashtray. No, he wouldn't go there.

The sky began to darken. Brad called room service and had a dinner tray brought up from the kitchen, a big platter filled with chicken and dumplings and fresh green peas and carrots. When it arrived, he sighed and looked down at it affectionately: he was going to miss farm portions when he went back.

The evening news came on. He noticed that Channel 1's coverage of Jemima's trial included his participation. He was surprised to see that somebody had grabbed a clip of him leaving the courtroom.

Wellman's smiling face reappeared on the screen. "It's unusual for a reporter to become part of the story," he smirked, "but Brad Williams of the *Ledger* newspaper has become an integral part of this remarkable tale. We're going to ask people on the street what they think of it."

He stuck a mic into a young woman's face. Brad sat up and scowled. It looked like Wellman had been shooting on the square in downtown Serenity.

The girl giggled. "I think it's romantic!" she chirped. "He's so handsome!"

Brad raised his eyebrows sardonically.

The reporter moved on to a young woman standing nearby. "What's your opinion? Have you heard about Jemima King's trial?"

"Oh yes." The woman looked like a college student and was quite pretty. "I loved that he came to testify for her. I think that was *wonderful*. He can come and do a story on me any day!" she laughed.

Brad shook his head and turned the TV off. *Great*. He was apparently the flavor of the month on the gossip circuit, which would explain some of Delores' recent emails. He made a mental note to tell her that she needn't think he was going to play into that if she was planning it.

The pool lights switched on below, and the ice maker down the breezeway kicked in with a *thrum* as somebody lifted the hatch and raided it.

Brad checked his watch. It was a little past 9 p.m., so he went to the bathroom to shower and shave and dress.

He might not know what he was going to say, but he *was* sure of one thing: he wanted to look his very best when he saw the Duchess for the last time.

Brad pulled his truck up to the spot where he always parked: a little wide space in the dirt road, next to a high bank. He switched off the headlight and pulled the keys out of the ignition.

He took a deep breath and peered through the windshield. It was a beautiful September night, crisp, but not too cold. The moon was a big silver dollar riding high in a dark blue sky, and was so bright that he could walk through the dark without a lantern.

He opened the door and got out. The pale silver light was enough to show the way.

He followed his now-familiar path: over a low split rail fence, into the overgrown field. The last crickets of summer chirped thinly from the bracken, and overhead, the sky was full of stars.

He threw a long leg over the low fence to the King farm, and hopped over, and through the bushes to his usual place. And Jemima was standing there, waiting for him.

He stopped to look at her. The white moonlight touched her with silver: it outlined her little cap, and her hair, it painted the delicate planes of her face, touched her nose, underlined her lips.

He tried to speak, and found that his carefully-considered speech had flown off to the sky. That he had no words.

So he just held out his arms.

To his amazement, Jemima King, the Amish millionaire, the girl whose beauty had enchanted the whole country, came running into them, threw her little arms around his neck.

And *kissed* him.

He stood there, too stunned for the moment to register anything except the luxuriant feel of velvet against his lips.

Then she pressed her cheek against his and held him. "You were so good to come to court," she whispered. "I will *always* remember."

He blinked. A heavy sensation in his chest made it hard to talk. *Oh, right. He was leaving.*

He tried to smile. "No worries, Duchess," he said, though his voice sounded odd, even to him. "I owe you. I'm glad things have turned out okay for you. You deserve to be happy. Have you – have you decided which of those three guys you're going to marry?"

She was still holding him, looking out over his shoulder. She shook her head.

He tried, for the sake of being kind – and he told himself that it *was* kind – to make a joke, to show her that she needed to get on with her life, just as he needed to get on with his. But for the first time in his life, he couldn't summon the right words.

She clutched his shirt. And just as she always did, she astounded him.

"Do you think I should marry one of them?" she asked.

He looked up at the sky in disbelief, then down at the

ground, and then down at her. The correct answer, of course, was: *Yes, you should. They're like you, they can give you what you want, they're part of your world, they understand you.*

But instead -- like a moron -- he shook his head.

Now she was trembling in his arms, like some beautiful, fragile bird. She whispered in his ear, something so soft he could barely make it out.

"Why not?"

Brad set his jaw, squeezed his eyes shut, and willed himself to do the right thing. He opened his mouth to say the right words, the kind words, the words that made sense.

Instead, to his horror, he heard himself saying: *"Because I love you, Duchess."*

Once the words were out, it was too late, too late to take them back, too late to tell her he'd made a hideous mistake, too late to do anything except receive the sweetest, wildest kiss of his entire existence, one that turned his brain to popcorn, made him forget everything, all his objections, all the obstacles, and even his own name.

Everything, in fact, except a brief confusion: he wondered why she was sobbing. But then she put her tiny fingers in his hair and kissed him again, and every question he had ever had flew away to the smiling moon.

THE END

THANK YOU FOR READING!

And thank you for supporting me as an independent author! I hope you enjoyed reading this book as much as I loved writing it! If so, there is a sample of the next book in the series in the next chapter. You can find the next book, An Amish Country Treasure 4, in eBook and Paperback format at your favorite online booksellers.

All the Best

Ruth

AN AMISH COUNTRY TREASURE 4

Though Englischer boy-wonder reporter, Brad Williams has declared his love for Amish teen, Jemima King, are they truly meant to be together? Or can another win Jemima's heart?

After having faced fame and a shocking lawsuit, Amish teen Jemima King now has the freedom to choose her future. But things are not as bright as they seem. Yes, boy-wonder Englischer reporter Brad Williams says he loves her, but does he love Jemima enough to respect her desire to live as an Amish woman – and join her? Or will one of her other Amish suitors find a way to win her heart?

And what about the money Jemima King has vowed to give away? Will she find the strength to follow through on her promise? Find out in An Amish Country Treasure 4 – the riveting conclusion to the Amish Country Treasure series.

CHAPTER ONE

Jemima stood, watching and listening, at the property line of her family's farm. She leaned against the fence as Brad Williams clambered over, turned to kiss her one last time, and slowly melted into the darkness beyond. She stood listening as the crunch of his footsteps grew fainter and fainter, until the distant growl of a motor and the faint nimbus of unseen headlights flared, faded and disappeared.

After he had gone, the midnight world was very still and quiet. A solitary owl purred in the distance. Further still, a very faint sound: a train whistle from the crossing beyond town.

Jemima smiled, looked up into the starry sky and hugged herself.

It was turning cool, but the feel of Brad's mouth still tingled in her own, the warmth of his kisses was still on her lips, her face, her neck. She was trembling slightly. She had never in her life felt so alive. Jemima closed her eyes and replayed every word Brad had pressed into her ear. The way he'd said *duchess* this time made her look forward to hearing it again.

But best of all, better than anything, Brad Williams—the

cynical, fast-talking reporter—had made himself completely, gloriously vulnerable.

He'd admitted that he loved her.

Jemima laughed suddenly, took her skirts in both hands and twirled around, making them billow out into the air like a blooming rose.

When she returned to the house, it was dark and still. There wasn't a light even in her parents' window, and the yard and the house were hushed. Jemima entered by the back porch. She opened the door softly, took off her shoes and crept up the back stairs, being careful not to make a sound.

The moon was as bright as day, slanting through the windows and hall floor. Jemima tiptoed past her parents' bedroom and the sound of her father's snores. She crept down the long hall, past Deborah's door. Jemima gave it a wary glance, but there was no light underneath it. Then she slowly twisted the knob to her own door, slid inside and closed it softly behind her.

Once she was safely inside, Jemima smiled and walked to the window. Under that dazzling moon she could see the whole countryside stretching out to the horizon. The dark trees were drawn in charcoal and the rolling hills in white chalk.

She unpinned her cap, unmade her bun and let her silken hair fall free. It cascaded over her hands, over her shoulders and past her waist in shining waves. She brushed it absently, and plaited it into a long braid.

Then she came out of her dress, letting it fall into a heap on the floor. She sat down on her bed, and unrolled her stockings, and tossed them away.

Jemima fell backward onto the bed and stared up at the moonlit ceiling, smiling. Against all odds, Brad Williams *loved* her.

She closed her eyes, savoring the memory. He'd *said* that he loved her. And it was true, she could *feel* it, she could *taste* it. He'd made himself vulnerable, he'd confessed his weakness against his own will. *Oh, Duchess* – the shuddering way he had said it, just before the insanity of those kisses – it was the cry of a man in love.

She knew it, she *knew* it, *she knew it.*

"Do you know what you do to me?" he had breathed into her ear. *"Do you know you make me lose my mind? I should never have come, I should have told you goodbye. This isn't right, it won't work, it will only make things harder in the end. I should leave..."*

But then he had kissed her like a madman, and pulled her into his arms, and had lost his mind again. And after all the sweet insanity, after the Englischer's wild kisses, after her confusion and his despair, she was sure of only one thing:

Brad Williams might have lost his mind – but he wasn't

leaving. He would be coming back, and back again, just as he'd done since the first day they met. Only this time, he wouldn't be after a story.

Jemima smiled again, and bit her nail, and dove under the covers.

The next morning Jemima was up bright and early, neat and trim and pressed. She hummed and smiled over her tasks as she helped make coffee and toast for breakfast. Her parents exchanged a knowing look.

Rachel came up behind her daughter, and slid an arm around her waist. "Well, *you* look happy this morning, Jemima!" she smiled, and kissed Jemima's cheek. "And I think I can guess why."

Deborah was sitting at the table and raised her brows and looked smug but said nothing.

Jemima received her mother's kiss and blushed. "I am, *very* happy," she agreed, and turned her attention to the coffee pot.

Rachel pursed her lips into a knowing smile. "I won't pry into your love life, Mima," she said primly, "but I expect you to tell your father and I *first* – if you have good news."

Deborah choked on her coffee and hacked horribly for a few minutes, but still emerged looking strangely amused. Jemima colored more deeply, and nodded to her mother and said nothing.

Jacob wiped his mouth with a napkin and added: "Well, now that all the nonsense is calming down at last, we can get back to normal. I'm going to clear the drive and put my anvils back in the shop, and about time."

Rachel set a plate of biscuits on the table and sat down next to Jacob. She looked at Jemima and added: "You'll be wanting to go to the bishop today, won't you, Jemima? You can make out a check to the community fund, and then you'll have the whole awful thing behind you."

She looked down mischievously, and smiled: "And certain *young men* will feel free to come calling, I expect."

Jemima sat down at the table and shook out a napkin. "I-I think I'd like to take a few weeks to just – just rest," she stammered. "I don't want to think about anything, right now. Everything has been so hard and – and *trying*."

Jacob looked at his eldest daughter sympathetically. "Yes, my poor girl, you *should* take a few weeks off to enjoy living like a teenager again," he told her. "This business has been more than an adult could've handled, much less a slip of a girl. You can take your time. Go to all the sings and frolics and games you please. Don't worry about the money, for now."

Rachel twitched her brows together, gave her husband a quick look and cleared her throat, but said nothing.

Jemima put a forkful of pancakes in her mouth, and was

grateful for her parent's merciful attitude. But she also noticed, to her alarm, that Deborah's amused eyes still watched her all throughout the meal...

THANK YOU FOR READING!

I hope you enjoyed reading this sample as much as I loved writing it! If so, you can find An Amish Country Treasure 4 in eBook and Paperback format at your favorite online booksellers.

All the Best,

Ruth

ABOUT THE AUTHOR

Ruth Price is a Pennsylvania native and devoted mother of four. After her youngest set off for college, she decided it was time to pursue her childhood dream to become a fiction writer. Drawing inspiration from her faith, her husband and love of her life Harold, and deep interest in Amish culture that stemmed from a childhood summer spent with her family on a Lancaster farm, Ruth began to pen the stories that had always jabbered away in her mind. Ruth believes that art at its best channels a higher good, and while she doesn't always reach that ideal, she hopes that her readers are entertained and inspired by her stories.

Printed in the USA
CPSIA information can be obtained
at www.ICGtesting.com
LVHW010058141123
763837LV00058B/553